"The first Christmas kiss of the season is good luck," he said, *pointing to the cluster of greenery that dangled above them.*

"Really?" Ruth said doubtfully. "I never heard of that tradition."

"Neither did I," he admitted. "I just made it up."

He touched his mouth to hers then, the movement brief yet decisive. And more than a little pleasurable.

When their lips parted, she met his gaze. Her clear, golden-brown eyes appeared to be smiling, as if she had enjoyed the kiss as much as he had.

The first Christmas kiss under the mistletoe. As far as he was concerned, it was indeed a lucky kiss.

He lifted his head to thank his lucky stars—and the little green ball of leaves that dangled over their heads.

"Oops, I was mistaken," he told her without a hint of remorse. "That's not mistletoe…it's holly."

Dear Reader,

Although it will be archived by now, I've been writing to readers on our www.eHarlequin.com community bulletin boards about Silhouette Romance and what makes it so special. Readers like the emotion, the strength of the heroines, the truly heroic nature of the men and a quick, yet satisfying, read. I'm delighted that Silhouette Romance is able to fulfill a few of your fantasies! Be sure to stop by our site. :)

I hope you had a chance to revisit *Lion on the Prowl* by Kasey Michaels when it was out last month in a special collection with Heather Graham's *Lucia in Love*. Be sure not to miss a glimpse into those characters' lives with this month's lively spin-off called *Bachelor on the Prowl*. Elizabeth Harbison gives us *A Pregnant Proposal* from our continuity HAVING THE BOSS'S BABY. Look out next month for *The Makeover Takeover* by Sandra Paul.

Other stories this month include the second title in Lilian Darcy's THE CINDERELLA CONSPIRACY. Be assured that *Saving Cinderella* has the heartwarming emotion and strong heroes that Lilian Darcy delivers every time! And Carol Grace has spun off a title from *Fit for a Sheik*. This month, look for *Taming the Sheik*.

And we've got a Christmas treat to get you in the mood for the holidays. Carolyn Greene has *Her Mistletoe Man* while new-to-the-line author Holly Jacobs asks *Do You Hear What I Hear?*

I hope that you enjoy these stories, and keep in touch.

Mary-Theresa Hussey

Mary-Theresa Hussey,
Senior Editor

Please address questions and book requests to:
Silhouette Reader Service
U.S.: 3010 Walden Ave., P.O. Box 1325, Buffalo, NY 14269
Canadian: P.O. Box 609, Fort Erie, Ont. L2A 5X3

Her Mistletoe Man

CAROLYN GREENE

SILHOUETTE *Romance*®

Published by Silhouette Books

America's Publisher of Contemporary Romance

To my agent, Ruth Kagle, who is beautiful on the inside as well as the outside. Thanks for believing in me.

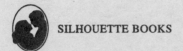 SILHOUETTE BOOKS

ISBN 0-373-19556-7

HER MISTLETOE MAN

Copyright © 2001 by Carolyn J. Greene

This edition published by arrangement with Harlequin Books S.A.

® and TM are trademarks of Harlequin Books S.A., used under license. Trademarks indicated with ® are registered in the United States Patent and Trademark Office, the Canadian Trade Marks Office and in other countries.

Visit Silhouette at www.eHarlequin.com

Printed in U.S.A.

CAROLYN GREENE

has been married to a fire chief for more than twenty years. She laughingly introduces herself as the one who lights the fires and her husband as the one who puts them out. They are a true opposites-attract type of couple and, because of this, they and their two teenagers have learned a lot about the art of compromise.

Coming together...mentally, physically and spiritually. That's what romance is all about, and that's what Carolyn strives to portray in her highly entertaining novels. Says Carolyn, "I like to think that after someone has read one of my books, I've made her or his day a little brighter. You just can't put a price tag on that kind of job satisfaction."

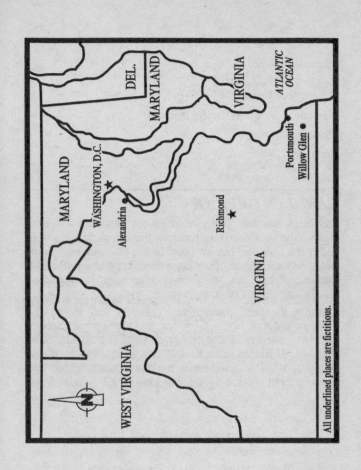

All underlined places are fictitious.

Prologue

The flashing neon light from the sign outside Tucker Maddock's Alexandria, Virginia, office window seemed to assault him in one-second intervals with its disgustingly cheery message.

Merry Christmas. Merry Christmas. Merry Christmas.

Yeah, right. He hadn't had a merry Christmas since…well, there was no need rehashing all the losses he'd endured during what was supposed to be the happiest season of the year. The overtime work did little to ease the discomfort that gripped him lately. As a corporate executive, he was one of the best decision-makers in the business. His troubleshooting skills frequently attracted the attention of corporate headhunters who regularly approached him with employment offers at competing companies. He only wished he could clear away the troubles in his own life as effectively as he did on the job.

Last year had dealt him the final and most difficult holiday blow when a Christmas Eve tragedy had taken the lives of Chris, his best friend, and Chris's parents. They'd been like his own family. And now he missed them. Wanted to be close to them. Wanted to fill the aching, gaping hole in his spirit with their memory.

Tucker stood and began clearing his desk. The flashing sign filled the semidarkened room with its alternating green-and-red eerie glow. The light seemed to pulsate within him, filling his mind and soul with its unwanted message. Filling his heart with an insatiable urge to be with the loving family who had opened their hearts and home to him.

The heck with this. If he couldn't be with them, he could at least return to the place that held their memory. Tucker dashed off a note to his secretary, then opened a drawer and swept his forearm across the surface of the desk, effectively clearing it of papers, folders and scribbled notes. He would sort them out when he got back. But right now, he couldn't bring himself to open another card, smile at another caroler or wallow in the home-and-hearth happiness that was supposed to pervade the season.

If he didn't get away from all the tinsel and glitter and glad tidings in the city, he was going to go crazy. And at times like this, he'd found it was best to follow his heart...follow it back home to Willow Glen.

Chapter One

He'd have to sleep somewhere. It might as well be here.

Willow Glen Plantation had seemed like a mansion to him the first time he had visited the massive house. It still impressed him with its sprawling front lawn, welcoming circular driveway, broad veranda, cheerful turrets and dormer windows. After spending the happiest times of his life here from age ten until college, Tucker had been devastated when Chris's parents sold the place shortly after he and his friend went off to college. Will Carlton, the county's antiques dealer, had done some minor remodeling on the home and turned it into a charming bed-and-breakfast inn.

An elderly gentleman, apparently just returning home from a Christmas shopping excursion, went in ahead of him and held the door for Tucker to follow him.

"If I were you, son, I wouldn't wait out here too

long. Dinner will be served soon, and believe me, you don't want to miss it.''

Inside, garlands and running cedar were strewn from every conceivable surface: the front desk, the mahogany banister rail that led upstairs, even the chandelier that hung from the parlor ceiling.

Although modern fixtures and a front desk, complete with an antique cash register, had been added, the place hadn't changed much over the years. It even smelled the same, like cranberries and pine and…what was that other smell? Tucker set his duffel bag down beside the curved-wood desk and closed his eyes while he inhaled the scent. In his mind, he could almost see Chris and Mr. and Mrs. Newland. He'd spent so much time in this house, sleeping here more than he'd slept at home, that he had become part of the family—so much a member of the family, in fact, that the elder Newlands had assigned him chores to perform. One Saturday a month, he and Chris were handed soft rags and a bottle of furniture polish to rub on the furniture, the banister and any other exposed wood, which constituted almost half the house.

He opened his eyes. That was the scent. Furniture polish. Maybe even the same brand.

An older woman, possibly more ancient than the gentleman who'd preceded him in, approached them. ''Oren, dear,'' she said, addressing the other guest, ''it's so good to see you again.'' She kissed his cheek, leaving a peach lip print on the gray stubble. Nodding toward the parlor where a group of guests had gathered, she added, ''Your wife has been anxiously waiting for you.''

The old man picked up his shopping bag and moved to join his wife.

Must be a regular, Tucker thought. The lady of the lip prints fixed her attention on him, scrutinizing him from head to toe and back again. "Well, aren't you a fine-looking young man. I'm Aunt Shirley," she declared.

That was a strange way to greet a guest, but he attributed the overfamiliarity to her advanced age. He gave her a warm smile. "Tucker Maddock, ma'am. I was hoping you'd have room at the inn for one more."

Aunt Shirley opened her mouth and laughed, the infectious sound attracting the attention of the people in the parlor. "He wants to know if we have room at the inn," she told them. They seemed to find it funny as well and laughed among themselves. One woman, a dark-haired beauty who appeared to be in her mid-twenties, caught his eye as she sat threading popcorn onto a string. Apparently feeling the heat of his perusal, she looked up. As they gazed openly at each other, Tucker felt the room grow suddenly warmer. He loosened the collar of his jacket.

A teenage girl followed the brunette's gaze and peered around the arched doorway at him. When she caught a glimpse of him, she blushed and drew back.

The brunette seemed to be studying him curiously from her overstuffed chair, as if he looked familiar to her but she couldn't place his face. But Tucker was sure they'd never met. If they had, he most certainly would have remembered her.

Her legs were drawn up beneath her in the chair. Long, slim limbs encased in charcoal-gray fabric that coordinated with the bulky gray-green top that seemed to swallow her small features. Her dark hair spilled in disarray over the plush material, bringing to mind an image of her cuddled in bed under piles of blankets.

Her brown eyes slanted downward at the outer edges, making her look as though she'd just awakened from a long, luxurious sleep, and her lips seemed to be made for kissing.

Tucker involuntarily drew the back of his hand across his mouth.

She watched his idle gesture and her chin came forward, causing her pale pink mouth to pucker invitingly.

Ruth pushed a wild and wavy strand of hair away from her face. She'd been working hard to make this—possibly their last—Christmas family reunion the best one ever. And this latest arrival, though unexpected, certainly promised to make it one of their most interesting family gatherings. The way the stranger's gaze roamed over her made her feel almost intoxicated. She tried to still the crazy inner stirrings that made her feel decidedly light-headed.

Stop that! she commanded herself. It was sick to lust like this over a family member, no matter how distant the ties might be. No matter how tall and broad shouldered he might be. No matter how touchable his collar-length brown hair was or how his dark eyes seemed to penetrate right into her and read her very thoughts. Dragging her gaze away from him, she looked across the room at her sister. Vivian hadn't yet noticed the newest addition to their family reunion.

Ruth smiled and returned her attention to the handsome stranger. He smiled back. This was one hunk her older sister wouldn't snag. Unfortunately, he was off-limits to Ruth, as well.

She considered getting up and joining her aunt in greeting the family members who came here from throughout the state to attend their Christmas reunion, a regular event since they'd bought the former hotel eight years ago. Though she'd grown up in Willow Glen, it wasn't until she'd moved into the old plantation house that she'd finally felt truly at home.

Aunt Shirley seemed to be holding her own. Now that the preliminary cleaning and cooking were done, she was in her element, reacquainting herself with family members from near and far.

Aunt Shirley turned back to Tucker. "You have such a wonderful sense of humor. Of course we have room. And we'd *make* room if we didn't."

"Uh, thank you, ma'am." He reached down and picked up his duffel bag. "If you'll point the way and give me a key, I'll just head on to my room."

"Call me Aunt Shirley. Everyone else does." She went behind the polished counter and refastened a paper Santa that adorned the wall. "As for keys, you don't need them here, honey. Nobody will mess with your stuff. Oren sleepwalks sometimes, but you can latch your door from the inside while you sleep."

Tucker frowned. He was familiar with mom-and-pop establishments, but this one beat all. However, room security shouldn't be a problem since he intended to be there the entire time. If the room didn't have a VCR, he could buy one and numb his brain with action-adventure movies for the holiday. Escape into the happiness of the past until the relentless false cheeriness of the season had subsided. As he faced his first Christmas alone, it would be just the medicine he needed to revisit the place that had given him so many happy memories.

"Maddock," Aunt Shirley said, rubbing the pale coral rouge from her left cheek. "I don't seem to recall any Maddocks."

Maybe she was asking if he'd been a guest at the inn before. Either that or she assumed—correctly— that he was from Willow Glen. In a town this small, everyone was either related by blood or marriage, or they went to school with one another. He wasn't surprised she didn't know his name. His parents weren't originally from here, having come to Willow Glen shortly before he was born. After his mother died twenty-some years ago, his father drank all their money away and they'd lived on public assistance.

But he wasn't going to tell Shirley all that. "I grew up not far from here," he said. "I haven't been back in more than ten years."

The brunette narrowed her eyes at this revelation and joined them in the foyer. The older woman's questions had seemed born of curiosity, but the younger one appeared somewhat skeptical.

"What are your mama and daddy's first names?"

He chalked the question up to her being a true Southerner. Tucker knew that many Virginians could be obsessive about knowing a person's lineage. So he humored her, glad for the opportunity to get a closer look at the lovely, gentle-eyed brunette as they spoke. "Helen and Bob."

He loosened the top few snaps on his jacket.

Oddly, as if she weren't aware of copying his action, she lifted her hand to the vee of her shirt.

Tucker's gaze followed her movement and lingered on the dip in her throat. He didn't remember this house being so warm.

Tucker forced his attention back to Aunt Shirley. She pursed her bright peach-colored lips, making the lines around them form a miniature starburst pattern. "We have a Helen in our family, but I don't remember any Bobs. Was Bob your mama's second husband?"

"Huh?"

Oren called from the parlor. "Leave the boy alone, Shirley, and come in here so we can get this tree up."

"Okay, okay. Just hold on to your knickers."

Tucker shook his head, amazed by the easy familiarity the hotel staff had with most of the guests. He assumed some of the guests liked it here so much they had become regulars. It could be that after a while they started to feel like family. Must be something about this house, and the love that lingered here, that gave people a sense of belonging, he decided.

"Come on," said Shirley. "I'll show you to your room. I hope you don't mind being on the third floor. I had considered putting in an elevator, but lately I've been thinking of more interesting ways to spend my money."

"That's okay, Aunt Shirley, I'll show him the way."

Although it would have been flattering to think the brunette's interest matched his own, Tucker got the distinct impression that she had another reason for offering to show him to his room.

She led him up the mahogany staircase to the third floor, pausing a couple of times after the first level as if to give him an opportunity to catch his breath. But he had no trouble keeping up with her. With a view such as she offered, he much preferred to enjoy it from close range.

Upstairs, Tucker stepped into the room, and it felt as if he had retreated into the past. He set the duffel bag on the floor and let the sensations wash over him. The curtains, handmade patchwork quilt and scatter rugs were different from his childhood recollections, but they retained the flavor of the era. However, the curved sleigh bed and matching chifforobe had apparently been included in the sale of Willow Glen Plantation. Bending closer, he saw that the tiny carved initials, R.T.M., for Robert Tucker Maddock, had remained. Mrs. Newland had blown a gasket when she'd seen what he'd done, but after giving it some thought she'd promised to let it stay. At the time, Tucker didn't understand his surrogate mother's change of heart. In retrospect, he saw that she had kindly allowed a scared, lonely boy to make his mark in her home, on her family and in her heart.

Apparently unwilling to relinquish her hostess duties, Aunt Shirley joined them in the small room. "It is so good to have you join us for Christmas."

The brunette responded with a tightening of her softly curved lips, walked past him and pushed open the white lace curtains to allow in the meager late-afternoon sunlight. When she was done she turned and scrutinized him thoroughly. After a long, uncomfortable moment, she reluctantly announced, "Yes, I suppose you do have the eyes."

He had no idea what the young woman was talking about, but he supposed that his features may have stirred up a previously forgotten memory of having met his father. In a town this size, most people knew everyone else, even if only in passing. ''People say I have the Maddock eyes,'' he said.

If he'd had a choice in the matter, he would rather forgo the dark, devilish feature that attracted so much attention than have even that one small remaining link with his deceased father.

Aunt Shirley stepped forward, her arms open, and took him in a motherly hug. Pressing a light kiss to his cheek, she said, ''We're so glad to have you in our family.'' Moving to the door, she added, ''If there's anything you need or want, just let one of us know, and we'll see that you're taken care of.''

With a wink and a wave, she exited the room and closed the door behind her.

The younger woman stayed where she was, arms across her chest, assessing him.

Still stunned by the older woman's unexpected gesture, Tucker stood rooted to the faded blue throw rug, absentmindedly lifting a hand to his cheek where she had kissed him, and wondered if the woman before him might follow suit. He sure hoped so. He had heard that these bed-and-breakfast places sought to make their guests feel like members of the family, but in his estimation, the elderly woman took this home-and-hearth stuff a tad too far.

The door swung open again, and Aunt Shirley popped her head in. ''I almost forgot…hurry and unpack. We'll be waiting for you downstairs to help put up the Christmas tree.''

He'd better nip this in the bud. If he didn't stop her now, she'd have him singing carols and baking Christmas cookies with the rest of the guests.

"Uh, Ms., I mean, Aunt Shirley, I'm not really up to trimming a Christmas tree this year." Although he was finding comfort in returning to the memories in this house, the Christmas traditions only served to remind him of all the loved ones he'd lost at this time of the year.

"Oh. It would present a bit of a problem if you don't join us. You see, Aunt Shirley isn't up to having a big crowd here after this season, so I'm trying to make this last one our best Christmas ever. It would really mean a lot if everyone would participate." The young woman looked thoughtful for a moment. "Would you rather put up the wreath or string Christmas lights instead?" The two of them seemed determined to have him participate in the festivities.

He sympathized with their business plan to cut back their tourist season. It must be difficult sacrificing their own Christmas activities in order to take care of a bunch of guests. But he still had no desire to change his plans in order to be with strangers. He solemnly shook his head.

Aunt Shirley grinned. "Holding out for hanging the mistletoe, eh? I figured you for a romantic, right from the start."

At the word *romantic,* his gaze veered back to the pretty brunette. Impulsively, he asked, "Are you going to help?"

"Of course," she said, as if the answer should have been obvious.

He scratched the whiskers on his chin and took in her fair, flawless complexion. "Maybe I can come down for a short while."

"Good," said Shirley. "I'll tell everyone to wait

for you.'' This time when she left, the older woman hooked the brunette's arm and steered her out of the room before her.

Downstairs, Ruth pulled out the dusty old Bible, her curious cousins, aunts and uncles gathering around her as they traced the family's lineage.

''He's cute,'' said fourteen-year-old Brooke.

''He's too old for you,'' Vivian stated, as if it weren't already apparent to everyone in the room. ''I'm sure he'd prefer someone closer to his own age. Like me.''

Ruth drew a finger down the page, searching for the Maddock name in the birth and marriage listings. ''You're both being ridiculous,'' she said without lifting her head. ''If he's a relative—which I doubt he is—he should be treated like any of our other cousins.''

Brooke giggled. ''Maybe he's a kissing cousin.''

Ruth pushed her hair behind her shoulders and tried unsuccessfully to ignore her young cousin's remark. ''Just as I thought. I don't see a record of a Maddock anywhere in here.''

Oren nudged her aside with his cane and bent over the book that lay open on the coffee table. He turned a page to the crowded family tree. Lilly Babcock, now deceased, was the matriarch of their close-knit family. Although Lilly and her husband Clem's daughters had married, introducing new surnames to the family tree, the subsequent generations still considered themselves Babcocks.

After a moment, Oren pressed his finger to a box with a line drawn from Ruth's great-grandmother Lilly. ''There's a Helen in here who married a third cousin, but I don't see any sign of a Maddock or her giving birth to a Tucker.''

Aunt Shirley joined them, leaning over the brittle pages. Her elderly boyfriend stood and moved beside her, taking her fingers in his own.

Ruth watched the exchange and was thankful once again that her aunt had found someone to love and who loved her so much in return. She hoped that someday she'd find a special man who made her as happy as Boris made Shirley.

The thought occurred to her that perhaps Boris was the reason Aunt Shirley had decided not to hold the Christmas family reunion again after this year. Such an event was an awful lot of work and planning, and it was understandable that her aunt would want to spend her time and energy on her personal pursuits. And that was why Ruth had stepped in and shouldered most of the hostessing duties this year. By making this their most perfect Christmas ever, she would relieve her aunt of much of the work while convincing her to give it a go again next year.

Their yearly reunion helped solidify Ruth's sense of family togetherness. Having lost her parents at a very young age, it was important to preserve and nurture her family ties. And someday she hoped to marry and add lots more names to their Bible.

Turning her attention back to the book, she recalled her great-aunt's earlier questioning of their handsome guest. ''Do you suppose Helen remarried, Aunt Shirley, and you lost track of her?''

''If so, that would mean Tucker Maddock is only vaguely—and very distantly—related by marriage,'' Vivian said with interest. ''A step-cousin, of sorts.''

Ruth didn't know why this possibility should please her so much. Or why it should bother her that her sister was so quick to pick up on their nonexistent blood ties.

"I don't know." Aunt Shirley idly rubbed the wattle of skin under her left arm. "I think Helen and her first husband are still together. But I could be wrong. I haven't heard from them since right after Brooke was born, which would be about fourteen years ago."

A trickle of concern flowed down Ruth's spine, leaving goose bumps in its wake. Even if Helen had divorced and remarried a Maddock after that time, there was no way she could have a son who, by Ruth's best estimate, was about thirty years old.

Ruth smelled a rat, albeit the best-looking one she'd ever laid eyes on. Although Ruth Marsh was normally an easygoing person—so easygoing, in fact, that her fourth-grade students had nicknamed her "Miss Marshmallow"—she could not sit idly by while some stranger with an ulterior motive invaded their home. Right in the midst of their Christmas celebrations, no less!

Like the rest of the Babcock family members, Aunt Shirley was a trusting soul, welcoming anyone and everyone into her life. In fact, it was that very generosity of spirit that had led the older woman to raise Ruth and her older sister after their parents had died.

Aunt Shirley had protected her when Ruth was a child, and now it was Ruth's turn to repay the favor. She would not let this situation untold like that roofing repair sham her family had fallen for. Or the unsecured-bond investment scheme Aunt Shirley had naively bought into.

"I don't know, Aunt Shirley," Ruth said. "Something doesn't seem right about this particular long-lost relative. For all we know, he could be another shyster, or even an ax murderer."

"Nonsense." Aunt Shirley disengaged her hand from Boris's grasp and closed the musty book. "I won't have you talking about your own cousin that way. In every family there are three horse thieves for every prince. Regardless of whether his branch of the family tree is represented on a coat of arms or has a noose hanging from it, he's still family."

She straightened and addressed Ruth with an expression that made it clear she hadn't learned the lesson taught by the roofer and investment crook. "I'm sure that nice young man has a perfectly reasonable explanation for his name not appearing in our Bible."

Ruth shook her head at her aunt's complete trust in other people. The older woman had a reputation around Willow Glen as being wealthy and more than a little eccentric. She hated to think that another unscrupulous person might try to take advantage of that trust.

"Cousin Tucker is a fine fellow," Aunt Shirley said, trying to reassure her. "Just give him a chance."

Give him a chance to do what? Rob them blind? Murder them in their sleep? It was clear she would get nowhere with her family, so she let the subject rest for now. With a few well-chosen questions, she would soon ascertain the newcomer's genealogical background as well as his intentions.

As Tucker came down the curved staircase, he saw the group huddled over a large Bible. They were probably reading the nativity story. He had serious doubts about his own sanity, agreeing to join in the Christmas celebrations when that was specifically what he'd been trying to avoid this year. If it weren't for the brown-eyed brunette, he'd be in his room reveling in a game of solitaire right now.

If he'd been a suspicious man, he would conclude that certain women have the ability to zap men with a mysterious pheromone that robs them of their reasoning powers. If that were the case, he must have been hit with a double dose of the stuff.

By the time he entered the parlor, the group had finished their discussion or prayer or whatever, and all turned as one to face him. Discomfited by their scrutiny, Tucker glanced down to make a quick assessment of his appearance: turtleneck tucked neatly into jeans, zipper up, and both socks matched. Nope, nothing wrong there.

When he looked up, they were still staring at him. Especially the brunette. Only she seemed to be studying him harder than the others.

The sandy-haired teenager with too much makeup spoke first. "Hey, cuz."

Tucker wrinkled his eyebrows. Cuz? He wasn't up on teen slang, but he hoped it was a compliment.

"Glad you could join us," said Aunt Shirley.

Oren spoke next. "She didn't twist your arm, did she? Shirley is the bossiest woman I've ever had the misfortune to know."

Rather than coming to her defense, the others smiled and nodded their agreement. Aunt Shirley smiled, too, as if she were proud of the distinction.

"No," Tucker said, "my arms are just fine." It was

his brain he had to work on. He had come here to be alone, so why on earth was he standing amid ten strangers with the intent of celebrating the very holiday he'd been trying to avoid?

"Good," said Aunt Shirley, "then you can climb that ladder and use those arms to string the electric lights on the tree."

"There she goes again," Oren griped. Turning to the proprietress of the inn, he added, "The least you could do is introduce him to everybody before you start bossing him around."

The brunette stepped closer to Tucker. "That's okay, I'll take care of it." Then she rattled off their names, pointing to each as she did so.

Aunt Shirley, he already knew, and her boyfriend Boris Schmidt. Then Oren Cooper and his wife Ada May. And their son, Dewey, who appeared to be in his fifties. Eldon and Rosemary Givens, and Brooke, their teenage daughter. The brunette's sister, Vivian Marsh, with blue eyes so enormous she reminded him of a Siamese cat.

And, finally, the brunette.

"I'm Ruth," she said, extending her hand.

Her hand was small yet strong. Just like the rest of her, he suspected. He couldn't help wanting to get to know her better. *Much* better.

"Any of these names ring a bell?" she asked, sweeping a hand to indicate the people she'd just introduced.

Schmidt, Cooper, Givens, Marsh. He didn't recognize the family names, but it had been a long time since he'd been home to Willow Glen. Even so, most of these people were older than his own thirty-one years, save the Marsh sisters, who appeared to be about his age or a little younger. And Brooke. Tucker shrugged, giving a gentle shake of his head.

A question niggled at the back of his mind. Assuming these people were all from Willow Glen, which was what Ruth had led him to believe by her implication that he should know them, why were they here instead of celebrating Christmas in their own homes?

Well, they'd been grilling him about his family. Now it was his turn to ask a question or two. "I've heard of people whose Thanksgiving tradition is to drive to the Checkered Tablecloth on the other side of town for a turkey dinner with all the trimmings. Is gathering at Willow Glen Plantation a new Christmas tradition around here?"

Ruth quirked her mouth, her lips pressing firmly together as if she weren't satisfied with his negative response. Or the question he'd lobbed at her. "Something like that," she said as if he should have known.

In the next few minutes, the previously tidy parlor was strewn with ornaments, bows, lights and tinsel. Ruth reeled out the seemingly endless strings of lights as he attached them to the tree. The task threatened to overwhelm him with memories of the Newland family decorating a fresh-cut tree in this room so many years ago. Stringing the lights had been Mr. Newland's job, and he and Chris had hung the ornaments while Mrs. Newland stood back and pointed out bare spots. The only thing that kept him from bolting from the room was the woman who stood at his elbow, patiently handing up lights. And every time their hands touched, he had to fight the urge to pull her to him and kiss her breathless.

All the while, she kept firing questions at him. The only explanation he could imagine was that she thought he looked familiar and was trying to establish how they may have first met.

He could have come right out and told her they'd never seen each other before this evening, but he liked the sound of her voice. Despite his earlier need for solitude, he found himself enjoying the company of the tiny woman with the giant curiosity.

When he claimed no knowledge of the various names she threw at him, her attitude seemed to change from curiosity to misgiving. Maybe she was finally figuring out that, although he might look familiar, they'd never met before today.

By the time they finished the tree, they'd settled into an uneasy silence. Tucker didn't know what had derailed their conversation. He didn't think he'd said anything out of the way. He'd tried asking her a few questions, like what part of Willow Glen she was from, but that seemed to make her even more edgy. So he turned his attention to the other guests and surprised himself by having a good time. For a brief while, the laughter and joking made him forget why he'd come to Willow Glen…and Willow Glen Plantation in particular. After the tree was finished and he'd helped put away the excess decorations, he excused himself and returned to his room.

Ruth watched him go up the stairs.

"The rear view is just as interesting as the front, eh?" Vivian teased.

"Yeah, but he has no business being here."

"Are you still on that?" Vivian put a hand to her perfectly styled bottle-blond hair. "Why can't you just leave the guy alone? He seems really nice. Very charming, if you ask me.''

''So did Ted Bundy, but I wouldn't want him crashing my family reunion.''

''Who's crashing our family reunion?'' Brooke demanded. ''Cousin Tucker?''

''He's not our cousin,'' Ruth insisted.

Brooke smiled broadly. ''Cool. I call dibsies on him.''

Ruth rolled her eyes. ''Don't be ridiculous. For all we know, he could be an escaped convict.''

''Or maybe he's with the Internal Revenue Service, and he's snooping around for unreported income,'' Vivian suggested. She smoothed her soft red sweater over her slim hips. ''I wouldn't mind him looking over my form. In fact, he can audit me anytime.''

Brooke giggled, but Ruth wasn't amused. ''You two may think it's funny, but something about that guy bugs me.'' He seemed to her like a man on a quest, but she wasn't sure what he wanted from them. She glanced up the stairs, wondering what would motivate a perfect stranger to insinuate himself into their home for the holidays. Well, the others might be willing to swallow the notion that he was a family member, but Ruth knew otherwise. And she was determined to get to the bottom of it. ''I'm going up there and see exactly what he's doing.''

Vivian laughed. ''Probably changing his clothes, if you're lucky.''

Ignoring the laughter of her sister and young cousin, Ruth mounted the steps, taking care to avoid the creaky ones. If Tucker Maddock was truly up to no good, she doubted he'd be so careless as to let her catch him at it. Even so, the least she could do was confront him about his identity and his intentions. She hadn't wanted to do so downstairs in front of the others, partly to keep from putting him on the spot in case he actually was related in a way she had overlooked, and partly because she knew her gullible family would rise to his defense even if he was an imposter as she suspected. After he'd charmed his way into her family members' hearts, joking and laughing while decorating the tree, they were convinced he could do no wrong.

As she climbed the last few steps to the third floor— the same level her room was on—she heard what sounded like something being scraped across the floor. Quietly, she made her way down the hall, glancing at the room numbers that remained from the house's brief bed-and-breakfast days. Ruth tapped lightly at the door of number nine. When no answer came, she turned the knob and peeked inside.

The room was empty.

Closing the door, Ruth went to her own room and checked to see if anything had been disturbed, but it looked the same as she'd left it earlier today. A glance around the empty hallway revealed that the attic door stood ajar several inches.

Ruth walked closer and saw that the attic light was on. Then she heard the sound again…a bump and a dragging scrape. Somebody was up there, and she had a good idea who it might be.

Moving quietly up the rickety stairs, she was at once shocked and yet not quite surprised to find their dark-haired houseguest running his hands over the loose floorboards where Aunt Shirley's trunk once sat. It was obvious he was searching for something.

Ruth placed her hands on her hips, enraged by the stranger's audacity.

"What do you think you're doing?"

Chapter Two

It was common knowledge in Willow Glen that Aunt Shirley had recently bought a new car with moldy money—cash that had apparently been buried somewhere on the property and retrieved when her dotty aunt was ready to make her purchase. Judging from the way Tucker had moved stuff around up here, it appeared as though he had heard about Aunt Shirley's odd banking habits and decided to make a withdrawal for himself. Just as she had suspected, he was not only a fraud, but an opportunist as well.

Tucker stood abruptly and cracked his head against the low attic ceiling. Rubbing the tender spot, he rumpled his hair, which made him look even more devilish.

Humph! The others might be swayed by his charm and good looks, but Ruth had learned to develop an immunity to such virtues, especially after Aunt Shirley had been taken to the cleaners by the fly-by-night roofing repairman and the so-called investment counselor. Besides, she had seen it all and heard it all, from adorable fourth-grade boys and girls who were adept at manipulating their parents and other adults into giving them what they wanted.

Ruth had a sixth sense about knowing when her students were up to mischief, but it didn't take a psychic to see that something was definitely off-kilter here.

"It's not what you think," he said, putting a hand up to the exposed beam he'd cracked his head against a moment before. He seemed to consider something for a moment, then asked, "Do you work here?"

"Do I *work* here? What kind of question is that?" Sure, she was working—especially this year as she sought to relieve her aunt of the burden of being hostess to so many houseguests. But he had asked as if he thought she were being paid to do her labors of love. Ruth climbed the remaining steps into the attic, but she didn't have to stoop as he did. "What I want to know is what you're looking for."

"Well, it's a long story, actually." Tucker wondered if he should go into the drawn-out course of events that had brought him here. When she hollered downstairs for Aunt Shirley to call the sheriff, he decided it would be prudent to start explaining. He paused, wondering how to begin.

"I'm waiting." Her toe tapped the rough board beneath her feet. Her arms were crossed over her chest, and he tried not to notice how that simple action enhanced an already admirable feature of hers.

Before he could begin, Eldon came galloping up the

stairs with Brooke hot on his heels. "Stay behind me, Brooke. I don't want you to get hurt."

He brandished a small pearl-handled pistol and scanned the close confines of the attic, his gaze skipping past Ruth and Tucker. He turned his back to Tucker, who was grateful to be out of range of the waving pistol, and faced the woman who had called for help.

"What's the matter, Ruthie? Did you see a mouse again?"

"No, I saw a rat," she said, pointing past Eldon, "and he's standing right behind you."

Brooke did an about-face and returned to the stairs. "Gross! I'm outta here."

Curious onlookers blocked her retreat. Tucker peered down the stairs as Eldon aimed the gun at Aunt Shirley's trunk. Sure enough, there in the hall stood Aunt Shirley and the rest of the guests.

Ruth tugged Eldon's sleeve in an effort to regain his attention. "I wasn't talking about a *rat* rat. I was referring to a *person* rat."

"Well, why didn't you say so?"

Once again, Eldon looked past Tucker as he searched for an intruder.

"Him!" Ruth stepped closer and patted Tucker's arm. "*This* rat."

Obviously confused now, Eldon stuffed the gun into his waistband. "Cousin Tucker? What'd he do?"

"Good grief, Ruth," piped in her older sister, "if you go with a guy to the attic, you really can't complain if he gets fresh with you."

Ruth sighed a huge breath of exasperation. "He didn't get fresh."

"Sounds like they need some *mesh*," said Boris from his vantage point in the hall.

Aunt Shirley patted his hand. "Turn up your hearing aid, dear."

By now, Ruth's face had turned a becoming shade of pink. Tucker wasn't sure whether that was from the cold or from her anger at having found him here. He rather liked Vivian's interpretation of the current scenario and briefly wondered if Ruth would consider an invitation to come back up here with him later. He looked over at her and saw that the sleepy expression in her eyes had been replaced by barely suppressed fury. Maybe now wouldn't be a good time to suggest such a rendezvous.

"I didn't come with him to the attic, I *found* him here." She pointed an accusing finger at Tucker's chest. "This man is an imposter. He came here, pretending to be a part of the family, just so he could rip us off."

"Family? What family?" Tucker took a step toward Ruth, ducking to avoid the noggin-hazard beam. When Eldon touched a hand to his waistband, Tucker figured he'd better start talking. Fast. "Look, I can explain everything."

"Great," said Ruth. "Then you can begin by explaining exactly where you fit into the Babcock family reunion."

"I don't know who the Babcocks are, or anything about their family reunion. I just came here for some peace and quiet."

"Ha!" Ruth whirled to face the others. "See, I told you he wasn't our cousin."

"You're right," said Vivian. "If he knew anything

at all about our family, he wouldn't have come here for peace and quiet.''

Tucker scratched his head and took a seat on the old trunk. ''You folks are all family?'' At their affirmative nods, he asked, ''Then what are you doing here at a bed-and-breakfast inn?''

The fiercely determined expression on Ruth's face dissolved into confusion. ''This place hasn't been a bed-and-breakfast inn for almost eight years.''

''But the Newlands, they sold it...''

''Right,'' said Ruth, ''and when the inn went broke three years later, Aunt Shirley bought it. We've been having our Christmas reunions here ever since.''

''You mean you're not our cousin after all?'' Vivian asked. Ruth could have sworn she saw an interested gleam in her sister's eyes.

Tucker shook his head. Now that Chris Newland and his parents were gone... ''I don't have any family.''

''And you're spending Christmas alone?'' Ruth asked, temporarily forgetting about his being a potential thief as she imagined him spending the holiday by himself.

''That was the plan.'' He rose from his perch on the trunk. ''I'm really sorry about crashing your reunion. I'll go gather my things and get out of your way.''

Aunt Shirley hollered up into the attic. ''Where will you go? The motels around here must be full.''

He leaned forward to peer down at the speaker. ''Yes, ma'am, they are. I'll just go back to my apartment in the city.''

"And who would you spend Christmas with?" Ruth asked.

Tucker shrugged. "I'll probably just go to work at the office. It's amazing how much you can get done when no one else is around."

"You're not going to spend Christmas alone." Aunt Shirley's words were an order. "You're going to stay right here and celebrate the season with us."

"That's very kind of you, ma'am, but I really don't belong here."

Ruth rubbed her arms to ward off the chill as she forced herself to remember that this stranger was an unwanted intruder. "You're right about that. And you still haven't explained why you were snooping through Aunt Shirley's attic."

"We're letting all the heat from the house up here," he said. "Why don't we go downstairs, and I'll be happy to answer your questions."

As the family members moved down the stairs, Ruth said to Eldon, "I think you should frisk him before he leaves this attic. There's no telling what he may have found before I caught him."

Tucker couldn't blame her for feeling this way. He'd be suspicious, too, if some stranger showed up on his doorstep and rummaged through his belongings.

"I ain't friskin' Cousin Tucker!"

Downstairs in the parlor, ten pairs of eyes studied the stranger who sat in their midst. They had just finished telling him about their initial assumption that he was a long-lost cousin. Now they were waiting for his explanation.

They were nice people. He doubted he'd be as understanding if someone had infiltrated his home. Ruth's reaction was closer to what his own would be, except that she didn't have the strength to pick him up and literally throw him out of the house. Instead, she sat there throwing daggers with her eyes. She was skeptical, and he didn't blame her. He plucked a strand of tinsel off the tree and toyed with it as he collected his thoughts.

"I started coming to Willow Glen Plantation when I was ten," he began. In the next few minutes, he explained how he'd come to consider the Newlands his family and this big old house his own. He'd thought that by returning here he could relive some happy memories.

Ruth still wasn't convinced. The others were hanging on his every word, but she'd learned not to take everything at face value. For instance, his claim of being a high-ranking corporate executive clashed sharply with the leather- and jeans-clad interloper who had barged uninvited into their home. What she couldn't understand was why the rest of her family couldn't see what she saw. And why hadn't they learned from Aunt Shirley's earlier bad experiences? "What about the attic?"

"I'm getting to that."

That piece of tinsel was getting wound around his fingers, weaving and curving in just the way she suspected the speaker was winding her own trusting family around those same fingers.

"Chris Newland was my best friend," he said. "He was like a brother to me. The year we turned eleven, we decided to make it official by becoming blood brothers. We signed a pact, put it in an envelope and sealed it with our blood.'' He turned to Ruth. ''That's what I was looking for in the attic. We hid it under a loose board.''

He seemed shaken. For a moment, Ruth's heart went out to him. But then she remembered that scam artists could be very convincing.

''So why, after all these years, did you finally decide to come looking for the envelope?''

''Ease up on the boy,'' said Aunt Shirley. ''Can't you see he's upset?''

And couldn't they see she was only trying to be prudent? Couldn't they see that *someone* needed to look out for the best interests of the family?

''That's okay,'' said Tucker. Although his words were directed to Aunt Shirley, his gaze met Ruth's and held it. ''If I were in her shoes, I'd be asking the same questions.'' Then, to Ruth, he said, ''I didn't come here looking for the envelope. As I said before, I came for some peace and quiet.''

He sighed deeply before continuing.

''Chris and his parents were killed in a traffic accident last Christmas. Seeing this big old house again brought back lots of memories, one of them being the pact Chris and I signed.''

Aunt Shirley stood, signaling an end to the interrogation. ''If you want peace and quiet, honey, then that's exactly what you'll get. You go on back up to your room. I'll give everybody strict orders not to disturb you. If you don't feel like coming downstairs for meals, just let me know and I'll bring 'em up to you.''

''Aunt Shirley!'' Ruth couldn't believe her ears. ''You can't let a complete stranger live in our house. You don't even know if he's telling the truth. He could have a criminal record or…or mental problems." Realizing, after the words were out, how they must have sounded, she said to Tucker, "No offense, but we've been burned before."

Oren took the sting out of her words by adding cheerfully, "You'll *know* he has mental problems if he chooses to stay in this house."

Tucker grinned. The bickering, the teasing, the noise and commotion…it all reminded him of the happy times he had spent with the Newlands in this house.

"I can't send him back to the city to work through the holidays," Aunt Shirley insisted. "Everybody's got to be somewhere at Christmas…he may as well be here. Besides, we have plenty of room."

"Yeah, Ruth," said Vivian. "Don't be such a wet blanket."

Judging from the look Ruth threw her sister, he doubted Vivian's words helped his case. Not that it mattered. No matter how enticing Aunt Shirley's offer might sound, he couldn't accept. It wouldn't be right.

On the other hand, his only other option—working through the holidays—was less appealing than remaining here. At home, he'd be miserable. He'd be miserable no matter where he was, but at least this was a change of scenery. And the best part of the scenery was the lovely young woman who was watching him as if he might steal the silverware.

He definitely wanted something from her, but silverware wasn't what he had in mind.

Aunt Shirley interrupted his hesitation. "I insist."

"Then I insist on paying regular hotel rates, and for the meals as well."

Tucker didn't know what made him agree to stay, but he suspected Ruth had something to do with it. It was nothing she said or did. More, it was a feeling he got from her. Although they came from different circumstances, he sensed they shared a common bond. He detected an undercurrent stirring her soul, creating a whirlpool of emotions in her inner being. As for himself, his whirlpool felt like a deep, black hole out of which he feared he'd never emerge. But, for some reason, that hole seemed a little less black, a little less bottomless, when he was near Ruth.

"We'll discuss that at checkout time," said Aunt Shirley, smiling. Then she mumbled something about making room at the inn in Bethlehem. The older woman seemed obviously pleased to have him join their household.

He could tell, however, that Ruth was not happy with the arrangement.

Ruth *wasn't* happy with the arrangement. She suspected the charming newcomer was up to no good, and she wondered why she was the only one who could see through this guy. But her family's willing acceptance of the stranger and their open invitation to him were thwarting her attempts to protect her impulsive aunt. Maybe he'd been telling the truth about the blood-brothers pact. But what if he hadn't been?

She got a stack of plates out of the cabinet and placed them around the table. When she was done with that, she returned to the cabinet for glasses. As she reached for the first one, a movement through the window over the sink caught her eye. A leather-jacketed figure was moving the two-seater convertible sports car to the carriage-house-turned-garage behind the house. Of course. He wouldn't want anyone ripping off his car while he ripped off her aunt.

He was convincing, that was certain. But apparently she was the only one who picked up on the subtle vibes that their handsome visitor sent out. Sure, Vivian and Brooke had picked up on some vibes, but she suspected they were more hormonal than anything else. Besides, Vivian picked up vibes from—and sent out signals to—all red-blooded males.

The message Ruth received from him was that he was a man on a mission. True, he was looking for something, but Ruth was convinced the "something" he sought was not a slip of paper under a floorboard. There was more. And she intended to find out what else he was after.

Ruth leaned against the sink and watched as he came out of the carriage house, pausing in the doorway to survey the grounds. Tucker was a devilishly good-looking man, no doubt about it.

Something brushed against her arm, pulling her back to the present.

Vivian nudged her with an elbow. "Want me to get a mop? Someone could slip and fall in that puddle of drool."

Ruth bristled at her sister's misinterpretation. "I just don't think he should have the run of the place. Who knows what he might be getting into?"

"Let it rest," said Vivian. "By the way, Aunt Shirley said to add another plate for dinner. She talked Cousin Tucker into joining us this evening."

By now, Ruth was gritting her teeth. "He's *not* our cousin!"

"Yeah. So?"

There was no arguing with these people. Once her headstrong family members had their minds made up, there was no changing them. And since, for the space of about forty-five minutes, they'd thought Tucker to be their cousin, he would forever after have that status. Talk about family ties!

Ruth got out another plate, and Vivian helped her carry the rest of the glasses to the large formal dining room.

When dinner was served, it turned out to be anything but formal. The noise and commotion were enough to make the Ringling Brothers envious. Aunt Shirley had to rap her tea glass with her spoon to quiet everyone for the blessing.

After grace was said, Brooke began filling Tucker in on who was who in their family, starting with Ada May. "Did you know Aunt Ada's a hooker?" she asked matter-of-factly.

Tucker glanced down the table at the sweet white-haired woman who appeared to be every bit of eighty years old. This was the one who, while they were decorating the Christmas tree, became embarrassed when Brooke casually used the word *pregnant* to describe the situation of a girl at her school. Ada May had hastily advised her young niece to say "in the family way" instead.

But now, having been called a hooker, she merely nodded sweetly, the flesh of her chin bobbing as she did so.

Tucker turned to the girl beside him and spoke in a low, unbelieving tone. "She used to do that, eh?"

"Still does," Brooke insisted. "Don't you, Aunt Ada?"

Ada May nodded again, making the flesh under her chin ripple like water on a rock-skipped pond. "I tried to get Oren interested in doing it, too, but it's not his cup of tea. He said the little bit of money I get out of it isn't worth all the effort I put into it."

Tucker frowned, trying to make sense of it. "You actually have...customers? And Oren doesn't mind?"

"Sure, I have them lined up waiting for my next piece," she said. "And of course Oren doesn't mind." She bestowed a loving look on her husband. "He likes to watch me work...says it's very relaxing."

"You're kidding."

"Oh, no, I wouldn't kid you. If you'd like, we can go into the parlor this evening, and I'll show you some of the tricks and fancy maneuvers I've learned over the years. I won't even charge you."

Tucker rubbed his chin, scratching the newly sprouted bristles. "That's, uh, very generous of you."

Sitting beside the elderly woman, Ruth smiled at Tucker as she patted her aunt's hand. "If you don't have time for a lesson," she told him, "perhaps you'd rather take a look at the assortment of rugs Aunt Ada has *hooked*."

Brooke giggled as the cat was let out of the bag. However, judging from Ruth's careful selection of words, it was clear they were not to let the elderly craftswoman know she'd been the butt of a naughty joke. She'd surely die of embarrassment.

Tucker took the hint and decided that changing the subject would lessen the chances of Ada finding out what was so funny.

"In that case," he confided aloud to the girl beside him, "I guess you could say I was once in a motorcycle gang."

"Really?" Brooke looked skeptical.

"Yep. When I was eight I joined a gang of kids who all wished we had motorcycles." He nodded thoughtfully. "We even got lick-and-stick tattoos."

Although Brooke rolled her eyes in the age-old tradition of teenagers, Tucker was rewarded with a smile from Ruth.

He liked her smile. He supposed it was the infamous Babcock smile since many of the people sitting at the table shared a similar feature. But hers was somehow different. Although her sister's smile was more stunning in an overt sort of way, Ruth's seemed to hint that there was quite a bit more to her than what showed on the surface.

And despite her understandable apprehension toward him, he wanted to get to know her better. Explore those marvelous Babcock lips. Make them turn upward with satisfaction like a cat that's had its fill of cream.

She averted her gaze and scooped up a forkful of mashed potatoes. Tucker watched, transfixed, as she brought it up to those full, lush lips that pursed to receive it.

"When's the last time you had a home-cooked meal like this?" Oren demanded.

Reluctantly, Tucker pulled his attention away from the lovely woman who had held him in her spell and turned it to Oren. He surveyed the blue china plate that was heaped with mashed potatoes, green beans, corn pudding, succotash, hot biscuits and meatloaf smothered in onion gravy. The last time he'd eaten like this was...well, when he'd been here with the Newlands.

"Oh, about eleven or twelve years, I suppose."

"You poor thing," said Aunt Shirley as she passed him the bowl of potatoes. "Eat up, dear. We have plenty. And there's pumpkin pie for dessert."

The rest of the meal passed in a blur, with everyone trying to get him to take more than his fill.

When everyone was finished, he picked up his plate as he'd always done with the Newlands and started to carry it to the kitchen. At the doorway, he paused. Emboldened by the family's unconditional acceptance, he considered the opportunity that presented itself. When Ruth, apparently unaware of his hesitation, collided into his back, he decided to go for it.

Recovering, she tried to peer around him. "What's the holdup?"

Turning around, Tucker took care to block the doorway to keep her from moving past the threshold. With a satisfied grin tugging at his lips, he met her questioning gaze and pointed to the cluster of greenery that dangled above them.

He glanced at the woman beside him to see how she was taking this obvious setup.

Not well. Her brown eyes flashed a warning at her giggling cousin, but it was too late. The rest of the relatives were now in on it and cheering them on.

Tucker flashed her his most encouraging smile. "The first Christmas kiss of the season is good luck."

"Really? I never heard of that tradition."

"Neither did I," Tucker admitted. "I just made it up."

The kinfolk behind them formed a semicircle to get a better look. Though Tucker found the idea of kissing her quite appealing, he would have liked it better if they'd been here alone.

"Just do it and get it over with," said Aunt Shirley. "If you make us old people stand here much longer, our varicose veins are going to explode."

Tucker looked at Ruth and gave a questioning shrug.

She returned with a resigned sigh. "We may as well do it, because they won't leave us alone until we do."

He took the plate from her and set them both on the sideboard. Then he lifted his arms, unsure whether he should hold her or just bend down and give her a little peck on the cheek. When she moved forward, face upturned and lips slightly puckered, he immediately discarded the latter idea.

Her arms hung by her sides, a clear indication that he was not to take this too seriously. He rested his hands on her shoulders. Although the bulky sweater made her look soft and round, her arms were lean and firm under his touch.

They each tilted to their right but still managed to bump noses. She looked away, embarrassed. While she was distracted, he touched his mouth to hers, the movement brief yet decisive. And more than a little pleasurable.

She tasted of sweetened iced tea, and her lips were warm, soft and surprisingly welcoming. Her eyes closed for an awe-inspiring second. For the briefest of instants, Tucker almost forgot they were surrounded by family.

When their lips parted, she met his gaze, all signs

of embarrassment gone. Her clear, golden-brown eyes appeared to be smiling, as if she may have enjoyed the kiss as much as he had.

The first Christmas kiss under the mistletoe. As far as he was concerned, it was indeed a lucky kiss.

Feeling magnanimous after his victory, he lifted his head to thank his lucky stars and the little green ball of leaves that dangled over their heads.

"Oops, I was mistaken," he told her without a hint of remorse. "That's not mistletoe…it's holly."

Chapter Three

Ruth didn't know why she had agreed to that stupid Christmas kiss thing Tucker made up a couple of days ago. At first she told herself it was because she knew her persistent family wouldn't leave her alone until she'd been manipulated into initiating the silly ritual.

But then, lying in bed later that night, she had to admit—if only to herself—that a tiny part of her had wanted to kiss Tucker. A *very* tiny part, of course.

Unfortunately, it did little to satisfy her curiosity, if that's what one called the strange little yearning that had invaded her well-being since ''Cousin'' Tucker's arrival. Instead, it was just enough to tantalize her into wanting a better sampling. It was like the nibble-size morsels of food they give away at the grocery store, usually at mealtime so the shopper can't get enough of the tasty fare.

And tasty fare he was. For a man as good-looking as Tucker Maddock, he was a surprisingly good kisser, especially considering the fact that he was holding back because of her family's presence. In her limited experience, she'd found that men of average appearance were usually better kissers than their handsome counterparts because they felt a need to compensate.

The tiny hairs prickled on the back of her neck. Maybe he was such a good kisser because he was compensating for some devious leanings. If he was truly a con man, he wouldn't want to leave anything to chance when wooing his next victim.

Then again, he may have just had a lot of experience.

In the three short days since he'd come to stay with them, he had managed to win over her entire family. Ruth had merely tried to keep a safe distance and a watchful eye.

Although Tucker made her uneasy by his presence, she was even more concerned when he stayed in his room and out of her sight as he had most of this morning. She'd found him in the attic once. Where might she find him next?

She got up from the sofa to throw the last log on the fire. It had been cold for the past few weeks, but last night the weather had turned bitter.

"Don't forget to bring in some more wood," Aunt Shirley told Boris. "Tonight's supposed to be even worse than last night."

As luck seemed to be having it lately—or perhaps it was carefully calculated timing—Tucker happened to be walking past the parlor as her aunt made her request.

He poked his head into the room. "I was on my way out to check on my car after I get something to drink,'' he told them. ''I'll pick up some wood while I'm out there.''

Boris, obviously relieved to be released from the chore, flashed his dentures at their houseguest.

''Why don't you get the wood while I fix you some hot chocolate?'' Ruth suggested. That way she could keep an eye on him through the kitchen window as she prepared the beverage, and perhaps she could learn some more about him as he drank it.

Tucker seemed surprised by her apparent change of heart. Nevertheless, he pulled on a pair of gloves and his leather jacket over his sweater and went out after showing a heart-stopping smile of thanks. Her heart turned a tiny flip at the seemingly innocent gesture, but she immediately tamped down the emotions that threatened her objectivity. She needed to be clearheaded when dealing with a pro such as Tucker.

Ruth got the tin of cocoa down from the pantry and stirred heaping spoonfuls into two mugs of milk. As they nuked in the microwave, she thought of all the things he'd done for her family since he'd arrived.

He'd played video games with Brooke and won, which highly impressed her young cousin. He'd tinkered under the hood of Eldon's truck in a show of manly bonding. And Rosemary was delighted by the fact that he'd cleaned the shower after using it.

Then he'd made a wholehearted attempt at rug hooking under Aunt Ada's careful tutelage. When Uncle Oren's cane had slipped on the polished floor, Tucker rooted through Aunt Shirley's stash of hardware until he found a new rubber tip to put on the cane. As for Dewey, who always loved a laugh,

Tucker spent the better part of an hour sharing his repertoire of jokes.

Ruth opened the microwave and stirred the steaming liquid. She thought of how Tucker had fixed a loose step on the back porch for Aunt Shirley and promised to take care of a curled corner on the parlor rug, cementing forever a place in her eccentric aunt's heart. And he'd gifted her sister with numerous compliments, a surefire way to win Vivian's devotion.

And now he was bringing in an armful of firewood for Aunt Shirley's boyfriend. There wasn't a single person in the family he hadn't sought to win over.

Except her. She didn't suppose the kiss counted, but considering the effect it had on her, it probably should have.

Prince Charming stomped onto the back porch just as she had finished setting the mugs on the table. Ruth dashed to the door and held it open for him to take his load to the parlor.

The bitter winter wind assailed her, and she quickly closed the door. When he returned to the kitchen, she was seated at the table, waiting for him.

If he suspected a grilling, he didn't show it. He merely peeled off his gloves and tossed them onto the table, followed by his jacket on the chair back. Ruth gave him the courtesy of waiting until he was seated before launching into questioning him.

Looking over his cup at her, he seemed to notice something. Even though she couldn't see his mouth, his eyes were definitely smiling at her.

"Why do I get the feeling I'm about to be sent to the principal's office?" he asked.

She picked up her cup. "Would you rather I leave?"

"Absolutely not."

Ruth didn't know why those two words should please her so much. If he was indeed a con man, he definitely had the right tools to do the job.

"The sixty-four-thousand-dollar question is, would you rather *I* leave?"

The words were spoken softly. He sounded so sincere, as though all she had to do was say so and he'd be out the door in a minute. Did he know that her family would practically disown her for turning away a guest? Was he banking on their allegiance...and Southern hospitality? If she sent him away, her relatives would work harder to make it up to him, and maybe even make some foolish mistakes in doing so. She doubted any of them would add his name to their wills, but she could imagine him being invited to weddings, the Fourth of July picnic, and myriad other family functions in the future.

"No, of course not."

She got up and brought back to the table a bag of marshmallows. Aunt Shirley was saving these for the sweet potato casserole on Christmas Eve. If her aunt complained, all Ruth had to do was say they were for Tucker's cocoa, and all would be forgiven. Even so, they wouldn't use many. Ruth wanted everything to be perfect this year, even down to the traditional casserole that her family liked so much.

He accepted one from the bag she offered him. The smile he gave in return was heart-stopping. "One's enough," he said. "I wouldn't want Aunt Shirley to take me out to the woodshed for snitching the marsh-mallows for Christmas Eve dinner.''

Ruth tried not to focus on the image of going out to the woodshed with Tucker. Instead, she fixed on the familiarity with which he addressed her family.

''You and Aunt Shirley seem to have taken a shine to each other,'' she said, stating the obvious.

If she didn't already have her guard up, she'd swear that the one-sided smile he gave was full of genuine affection.

''It's hard *not* to like your aunt.'' His gaze grew distant as he stared over her shoulder and out the window. ''When I'm here, everywhere I look is a memory. Even your family reminds me of the people who used to live in this house.''

''You talk about the Newlands as if they were your kin.''

He nodded. ''They grew up before the days of disposable diapers and dishes. They could never get used to the throwaway mentality of people who bought that stuff.'' He pushed the marshmallow down into his chocolate as if trying to drown it. The hooded appearance of his deepset eyes suddenly seemed more pronounced, and a muscle in his jaw tightened. ''Their attitude carried over to children. If a piece of furniture or equipment was broken, Mr. Newland would fix it. There was no way they would do any less for a human being,'' he said with a tight smile. ''They didn't believe I was ready for the trash heap.''

Ruth's heart went out to him. Suddenly, she didn't feel like continuing her planned interrogation. In her job, she often comforted students for everything ranging from poor test grades to the divorce of parents.

She frequently ignored the school administration's warning to avoid physical contact with her kids, preferring to give a motherly hug when needed. And the children repaid her by trying harder in their schoolwork and misbehaving less frequently in the classroom. The other teachers thought they called her Miss Marshmallow because she was a pushover. But one student had confided it was because she was sweet and tender…like a marshmallow.

Some strange impulse now compelled her to take him in her arms and hug him until the pain went away. In this case, however, Ruth suspected her fellow teachers were right. She was a pushover.

She resisted the urge but impulsively reached out, her fingers touching his big rough hand.

He looked up, his hand closing briefly around hers. Somehow, it seemed as though the gesture did more to comfort Ruth than the other way around. He was telling her, "It's okay. Don't worry about me."

But she couldn't help doing so. If she were being stalked by a wounded lion, she would still worry about the animal. And although the man sitting across from her with the dark lion's mane of hair was much like a wounded predator, she couldn't help worrying about him, either.

The doorbell rang, jangling them from their private thoughts. A moment later, Brooke appeared in the doorway. "There are some people here to see you."

Tucker watched a perplexed scowl cross Ruth's face and decided that, no matter what expression she wore, her features were an ever-changing work of art.

Curious, he and Brooke followed her out to the foyer. A young couple who looked older than their actual years waited with a boy of about ten or eleven and a little girl about half his age.

Like her parents, the girl was blond and fair-skinned. The boy, with his dark hair and olive complexion, reminded Tucker of a childhood photo of himself.

"Nicky!" Ruth rushed forward and took the boy in an affectionate embrace. After only a second's hesitation, the kid returned the hug. When she released him, she flashed the girl a warm smile and a conspiratorial wink.

"Mrs. Marsh, we're so sorry to interrupt you and your husband," she said with a nod toward Tucker, "during your Christmas vacation."

Behind him, Brooke barely suppressed a giggle.

Tucker cleared his throat and took a distancing step away from his supposed wife. "I'm just a friend of the family."

Ruth twisted her mouth to one side, as if she hadn't decided yet whether his words were true.

"You're not disturbing us at all," she said to the woman. Then, quickly covering her moment of doubt, she began the introductions. "Tucker Maddock and my cousin, Brooke Givens, this is Nicky Bartucci, a former student of mine and his parents..." She paused to allow them to supply their names.

"Charles and Natalie Johnson," the mother said. She dropped her hands to her blond daughter's shoulders. "And Nicky's little sister Angela."

The different last names explained the boy's dark good looks. Getting involved with yet another family was the last thing Tucker wanted to do, but his attention was drawn to the boy whose serious expression seemed out of place on his young face. He was curious about the kid. And that curiosity compelled him to stay and find out why the group had dropped in unannounced.

As they all shook hands in greeting, Tucker was thankful the rest of the Babcock clan was occupied elsewhere. He didn't even want to imagine the grilling Aunt Shirley would give them.

"We've recently found out about a wonderful employment opportunity for Charles." Natalie's voice seemed pumped with false cheeriness. "Only problem is, it's out of state."

Ruth pushed her hair behind her shoulders. It seemed clear there was more to the story than Mrs. Johnson was letting on. "Brooke, why don't you take the children into the parlor and show them our Christmas tree?"

To her surprise, her cousin readily agreed. Tucker, on the other hand, crossed his arms over his chest, making it clear he would not be dismissed from this conversation. A warning note went off in Ruth's mind. A really good con artist would want to know the family's business inside and out. Was he planning to use this information to his own advantage?

After the children had left the room, Charles spoke up. "Actually, I got laid off from work. If I can get this factory job in Kentucky, it would answer all our prayers."

Tucker spoke up. "Why don't you come in and sit down? We could go to the kitchen where it's private."

At first, Ruth felt embarrassed for having forgotten her manners. She smiled her gratitude to Tucker for trying to make them feel welcome. "We were just having some cocoa," she added. "You're more than welcome to join us."

"Thanks, but Charles left the car running." Natalie looped her arm through her husband's. "I realize it's short notice," she said apologetically, "but we were wondering if you'd mind watching the kids for a couple of days."

Charles patted his wife's hand. "Just long enough for me to go through the interview process and Natalie to look for a place for us to live."

"We've already asked all our friends," Natalie said, "but the ones who aren't laid off and busy looking for new jobs are trying their best to hold on to the ones they have. Then Nicky mentioned his favorite teacher, and we took a chance that you might be home during the school break."

Ruth took a deep, steadying breath. All her plans for a perfect Christmas were biting the dust, first with the arrival of Tucker and now with two kids who were most certainly feeling their parents' anxiety. But the Johnson family's Christmas plans were going far worse than her own. There was no way she'd turn them down, but she'd have to figure the logistics of adding two more people to the mix. Thinking out loud, she touched a finger for each item on her to-do list.

"Let's see, I've already taken care of Aunt Shirley's grocery errands and helped Rosemary with her Christmas shopping. But I'm not sure what the family has planned for the day after Christmas...."

"We'll be back the day before Christmas Eve," Natalie promised.

Ruth darted a glance at Tucker and found him wearing a scowl that made him seem dark and foreboding.

Supposing that his frown indicated his objection to having the children stay with them, she grinned. A wickedly clever thought occurred to her.

"We'd love to have Nicky and Angela stay with us for a couple of days," she said, flashing a triumphant smile at her unexpected houseguest.

There, let him deal with that. If he didn't like having a couple of active kids around, then maybe he'd pack up his bags and return to wherever he came from.

The looks of relief on the couple's faces was immense. Natalie gave Ruth an impulsive hug, and while she went into the parlor to say good-bye to the children, Charles stepped outside and retrieved the overnight items they'd left on the porch. Tucker took the shopping bags filled with the children's clothes and set them by the stairs.

After the parents left, he took his first long look at the boy. Once again, he was startlingly reminded of himself at that age. Though their features were nothing alike, other than their dark hair and complexion, it was the expression in the boy's eyes that could have made him swear he was staring at his own childhood image.

Nicky stared back, assessing him carefully.

"Nick, honey, why don't you help Mr. Maddock carry your bags up to your room?"

"You can call me Tucker," he said, extending his hand. The boy hesitated only a few seconds before placing his smaller hand in Tucker's.

"Tell them who I am," said a little voice from behind the boy.

Nicky moved aside and urged the girl to stand beside him. "This is my sister, Angie," he said. "She's five."

Angie popped her thumb into her mouth and spoke around the appendage. "Almoth thixth."

"That's pretty old." Tucker stooped to her level. "Are you married yet?"

Angie giggled, the happy sound worming its way inside his heart.

Ruth couldn't help smiling at the little girl's reaction to him. Despite her own earlier hope that the kids would scare him off, she begrudgingly conceded that he had a way with children. Irrationally, her thoughts leaped to the future when she'd be sharing moments like this with the father of her own children. She hoped that man would have Tucker's easy assurance with their little ones.

He stood and gave Angie a smile that was guaranteed to make any red-blooded female melt. And, sure enough, Angie fell head over heels for the stranger, wrapping her arms around his leg and giving him a tight hug. Tucker stroked her hair, his big fingers gentle and soothing.

For one brief, foolish second, Ruth wished she were the one he was touching.

"How old are you?" Angie asked, tilting her head back to look up at him.

He glanced over at Ruth, caught her watching, and winked. Ruth didn't know why, but that little gesture seemed to bond them.

"Thirty-one," he responded.

"How old is *she*?" Angie pointed at Ruth.

Tucker looked at her, studying her in exaggerated fashion for the girl's benefit. He cocked his head to one side and laid a finger against the shallow cleft in his chin as he appeared to be judging her age. Most people guessed her to be older than her twenty-five years. Not that it mattered, but she was curious about his perception. Finally, he turned to the child and stated with assurance, "She's old enough to be your teacher."

His vague answer was enough to satisfy Angie's curiosity. Ruth gave Tucker an approving smile.

"Where are they going?" Angie asked as she watched her parents get into their car.

Tucker answered for Ruth. "Your daddy's going to look for a new job. You and your brother will stay home with us until they get back the day before Christmas Eve."

Ruth couldn't help noticing his familiar reference to Willow Glen Plantation as "home." As if he were a permanent resident. An hour ago, his words might have bothered her...might have reminded her that he was an outsider who was getting in too thick with her family. Now, however, the words sounded comforting. As if he would be there for them.

He turned to look at her, sadness filling his dark brown eyes. When he put his arm around her, giving her a spontaneous hug, she could feel the tension in his body. Tension that had something to do with the children, but she could tell it wasn't about having to share the house with little people. There seemed to be something deeper causing his disquiet.

Aunt Shirley interrupted her thoughts when she stepped into the foyer. "I almost forgot," the older woman said to Tucker, "I hope you have something nice to wear to the Foutches' Christmas party tomorrow night." To Ruth, she added, "Tina called a little while ago to remind you that it starts at eight, so I told her you'd be bringing Cousin Tucker.''

The look her newfound ''cousin'' shot her said more clearly than words that he felt as awkward as she with this unexpected invitation.

To Ruth's surprise, Tucker spent the rest of the morning engaging the children in games such as hide-and-seek and red rover. He explained his involvement as an effort to distract them from their parents' absence.

Perhaps it was the look in his eyes when he first saw the children and heard about their family's predicament that convinced her he was a man of honor. Or perhaps it was the gentle authority he displayed with them that told her he was a man who respected decency and fairness.

Some people could fake charm. Some could fake their motives. But Ruth knew in her heart that this gentle stranger was not faking the qualities she saw in him.

She no longer feared him. She feared *for* him. She still didn't fully trust him, but something had changed upon Nicky and Angie's arrival. Just as he couldn't hide the concern he felt for two children he'd never met before, he couldn't hide that something was hurting him deep down inside. And, worrier and nurturer that she was, Ruth wished she could help him find the answer to whatever tormented him.

She laid her hand on his arm, wondering if the pain that he battled inside would eventually make his heart as hard as the muscles in his thick forearm. She'd seen how deeply the Johnson family was suffering in the midst of their financial dilemma, and she'd seen a different kind of suffering in Tucker's eyes. It frustrated her that there was no quick fix for any of the three visitors to her home. Squeezing her eyes to discourage the tears of sympathy that threatened to overwhelm her, she tried to express her gratitude.

"I—I want to thank you...for all you've done today." Unfortunately, her voice cracked, betraying her emotions.

"Hey, there's no need for that," Tucker crooned. In one smooth motion, he gathered her into his arms and pressed her head against his chest.

Though something told her she was crazy for doing so, she allowed herself to melt into his embrace, slipping her arms loosely around his waist. It was a safe, comforting feeling. Being held in his strong arms and feeling the hardness of his chest against her cheek made her feel pampered and cherished even though he was the one who seemed to need comforting. His hand remained against her head, and she felt his fingers twine through the rumpled texture of her hair.

So often Ruth had to be the grown-up. At school with her students, of course. And lately at home with Aunt Shirley, who didn't always use the best judgment. However, she was beginning to think Aunt Shirley's judgment of Tucker Maddock may not have been so terribly wrong, after all. For right now, it felt good to let someone else be the adult.

And he didn't disappoint her. With the flat of his hand, he rubbed circles on her back. When he spoke, Ruth enjoyed the rumble of his chest.

"We need to take the kids shopping," he said.

Ruth lifted her head. "For Christmas presents?"

''For clothes.'' His brown eyes seemed to darken. ''We can't let them run around in those rags.''

He was right. She recalled that, all last year, Nicky had come to her class in mismatched or ill-fitting clothes. ''Didn't they have anything decent in the spares they brought with them?''

He made a disgusted noise. ''Everything was ragged or too small. I think we should get them at least two outfits apiece, maybe three, from underwear to outerwear. And that includes shoes and coats.''

Ruth hadn't budgeted for such expenditures. But he was right. The children needed the clothes, and there was no question about whether she would buy them. She did a bit of mental figuring and decided that if she cut back on Christmas gifts to the rest of the family, she would be able to afford it. Barely.

Tucker's hand had stopped the gentle circular motion on her back, reminding her that the moment had passed. She straightened, pulling away from the comfort of his warm embrace. If he'd suggested this purchase as recently as yesterday, she would have wondered about his motives. But things had changed since yesterday. And that thought pleased and worried her. ''I'd better go get my checkbook.''

His expression tightened. ''When I said 'we,' I meant you shop, I pay.'' Her confusion must have shown, for he added, ''I don't know anything about buying clothes for kids.''

''That's so sweet. Thank you.'' Impulsively, she leaned close to him to kiss him on his cheek. But, to her surprise, he returned the gesture, this time on her lips.

The kiss lasted no more than a second or two, but

that was long enough for her to notice the soft firmness of his lips and the slight stubble that rubbed her chin. He received her kiss and returned it with a gentleness that made her long for more. Much, much more.

Footsteps in the hall broke them from their moment of tenderness.

"Well, well, what have we here?" Vivian smiled and placed one hand on a well-curved hip. "I was wondering if you needed any help settling the munchkins into their rooms, but it looks like you two need a room of your own."

Tucker stepped away from Ruth. The action could have been nothing more than an effort to lessen her embarrassment. Or it could be that the cycle with her sister was starting all over again.

Vivian looked great, as always. She knew she looked good, and she had always made the most of the very feminine attributes she'd been blessed with. Today was no exception. Her sister's blond-streaked tresses were perfectly complemented by the bright teal tunic top and matching leggings that showed off her slim legs to their best advantage. Although the tunic was meant to be oversize, Vivian had removed the possibility of looking baggy by adding a belt to the ensemble. She looked absolutely voluptuous. In comparison, Ruth felt dowdy in her black sweatshirt with its prim flower-embroidered collar.

Va-Va-Vivian, the boys had often called her. Or the Vampire Vixen. The nicknames were well deserved. And more than one of the boys that Ruth had brought home eventually wound up dating her more desirable older sister.

Well, Ruth wasn't dating Tucker, and she had no

intention of starting. So if Vivian wanted him, he was all hers. Ruth tried to squelch the selfish little feeling inside that hoped her sister wasn't interested in their houseguest.

Ruth cleared her throat. "We were just going downstairs to get Nicky and Angie some lunch."

Vivian practically purred. "I may be ten months older than you, little sister, but I don't need glasses yet. You two may have been cooking, but it wasn't lunch that was getting hot."

At the word *lunch,* Nicky and Angie had raced down the stairs ahead of Ruth. She had expected Tucker to accompany her down to feed the kids, but he stayed behind murmuring quietly with Vivian.

Ruth tried not to let it hurt her. After all, it wasn't a betrayal if she and Tucker didn't have an understanding between them. The most they shared was an interest in the children. But that wasn't cause for a romantic relationship. Oh, sure, there were a couple of kisses between them. The first—under the holly berries—had been something between a dare and a tradition. As for the more recent kiss, she had instigated it and she'd most likely read more into his response than he'd ever intended.

So why did she feel this huge letdown?

The only thing she could chalk it up to was competition. Vivian had always been older, better-looking and more charming, and she always got her way. For as long as she could remember, Ruth had tried to top her sister. But no matter how hard she tried, she'd always be the baby, the plain one, and there was no way she'd ever be as glib as Vivian. She'd always be second best.

Ruth paused at the bottom of the stairs. Second wasn't so bad. Of win, place and show, it was comfortably in the middle. And it was a far cry better than "also ran." Maybe she should just accept her second-place status in this family, stop competing, and get on with her life.

A few minutes later, after Ruth had the children settled at the table, Tucker walked into the room. As Brooke moved past him to leave, she turned and grinned at him. "Hey, Cousin Tucker, looks like Aunt Shirley got hold of you."

Ruth set the plate of grilled cheese sandwiches on the table and absentmindedly waved the children's hands away. She was more intent on watching Tucker's reaction as his dark eyebrows drew together at Brooke's comment.

"You have Shirley marks on your face," Brooke explained. When he still didn't understand, she spoke louder, as if the lack of understanding came from a lack of hearing. "The lip prints on your cheek. Shirley left her mark on you."

"Oh." Tucker gave a half smile and put a hand to his face. He waited until after Brooke had left before meeting Ruth's embarrassed gaze.

Angie was fascinated by the faint imprint on his face. She climbed up on her knees in the chair to watch as he slowly rubbed his fingers over the area. "Are you wiping it off, Cousin Tucker?"

"He's not your cousin, dopey," Nicky chastised. "You're supposed to call him Mr. Maddock or

Tucker, depending on which he prefers. Right, Ms. Marsh?''

Taking her eyes off Tucker's handsome face, Ruth turned her attention to Nicky as she placed bowls of steaming tomato soup on the table and rewarded the boy with a smile. "So you *were* paying attention in my class last year, after all, weren't you?''

"But everybody else calls him Cousin Tucker," Angie insisted.

Tucker sat in the chair beside the little girl and stroked her wispy blond hair. "We're not really cousins," he explained, "but if that's what you want to call me, it's fine with me."

She smiled with all the charm of an adorable five-year-old, then followed by sticking her tongue out at her brother. Turning back to Tucker, she asked, "Did you finish wiping the Shirley mark off your face?''

He flashed a crooked smile at Ruth, who almost spilled the milk she was pouring. She mentally chastized herself for letting the glance of this near-stranger have such an effect on her.

"I rubbed it in," he whispered to Angie in a voice loud enough for them all to hear.

Ruth felt her heart do a strange little flip-flop at his reaction to the kiss she'd bestowed on him earlier.

"Why?" Angie whispered back.

He grinned again. "Because I like getting kisses from pretty ladies."

Ruth dropped the spoon she was holding. It landed with a splatter in her bowl, and she covered her discomfort by focusing her attention on blotting the red soup off the tablecloth.

"Aunt Shirley?" Nicky said, incredulous.

Angie jumped up and down in front of him, determined to hold his attention a little longer. He must have that effect on all females. "Am I pretty?"

That was Ruth's thought exactly. For a brief moment she felt flattered that he would suggest, even indirectly, that he considered her attractive. But then she remembered that he'd dawdled in the hallway with Vivian when she and the children came downstairs. Were those her sister's lip prints? She hadn't paid close attention to the shade when Brooke first mentioned it, and now that it was rubbed away, she would never know.

Suddenly she felt worse.

"You're beautiful," Tucker said quite sincerely. For one crazy second, Ruth thought he was talking to her, and her heart leaped at his words. But when Angie beamed her delight from across the table, she remembered that her young ward had solicited the statement from Tucker.

Angie threw her arms around Tucker's neck, almost knocking over her milk in the process, and plastered his face with childish kisses. Ruth couldn't help smiling as he hammed it up, pointing out a spot on his chin that the girl had missed.

She imagined herself touching her lips to that fascinating cleft in his chin and being rewarded with a sultry-eyed look that told her she was the central focus of his thoughts. She imagined him cherishing her as a husband cherishes his wife, and a sense of longing swept over her. Longing for family, fulfillment and forever.

And that was when she realized what would make this truly the most perfect Christmas ever. A man to call her own. A man with whom to start a family.

"Yuck," said Nicky. "Let's eat."

Chapter Four

The children couldn't have been happier with their new clothes. That simple fact warmed Tucker's heart more than he would have liked.

As much as he hated to admit it, he was quickly becoming fond of Nicky and Angie. If he didn't watch his step, he'd soon find himself worrying about the little rug rats and checking on them after they left Willow Glen Plantation.

While Ruth helped Angie try on a pair of shoes the child didn't like, he plucked a pink-and-purple pair from the shelf. She'd been drawn to the sneakers as soon as they walked into the shoe department, but Ruth was trying to talk her into a less-expensive pair.

"Try these on," he said, dropping the shoes in front of them. "I think the little lady would look pretty in these colors."

Angie wasted no time pushing the unwanted pair aside and thrusting her tiny feet into the coveted shoes.

Ruth looked up at him, her eyes questioning. "They cost twice as much as the ones I was showing her."

"If it makes her happy," he declared, "then it's worth the cost." It was odd, but it felt like this was a tiny installment toward repaying all that the Newlands had done for him. And the feeling pleased him.

"You've already done so much," she protested. "Are you sure?" She had tried to pay for the clothes they'd bought earlier, but he had refused to allow her to do so.

Nicky, who'd been quiet through most of their shopping spree, sat on a bench waiting for his response. The look he saw in the boy's eyes reminded him of the first time he'd shown up at the Newlands' home to visit with Chris. The family had been about to leave for a day at a nearby theme park. He had fully expected Chris's parents to send him home so they could be on their way, but to his surprise, they had invited him along. Although he hadn't carried a penny with him, they paid for his park ticket, bought his lunch, and even made sure he went home with an armload of souvenirs.

He had always wondered what had compelled them to open their hearts, home and wallet to a kid like him. And now, looking at the wary, hopeful expression on Nicky's face, he began to understand what the Newlands may have seen in him.

"It's my early Christmas present," he said in an offhand manner intended to discourage any argument. "Hey, Nicky, what are you waiting for?" he asked, then pointed to the shelf behind the boy. "Those FastroLites are calling your name."

Ruth's mouth lifted on one side, but he wasn't sure

whether she was perturbed or pleased with him for spoiling the kids. It didn't matter. He got a tremendous charge out of watching Angie prance up and down the aisle in her new shoes. Sitting down beside Nicky, he picked up one of the battery-lit sneakers and started threading the laces through the holes.

A moment later, a couple with three kids moved past them and began the process of trying on shoes for the two older boys who were close in age to Nicky and Angie. The baby—a girl, judging by the pink jumpsuit—was hoisted on her father's shoulder as the mother pressed her thumb against the boys' toes to make sure they had growing room. Except for the baby, the family reminded him of Ruth, himself and their temporary children.

And the thought scared him. Here he was thinking and acting like a family man, when all along he'd only wanted to get away by himself for the holidays.

The man with the baby turned and smiled at him in recognition. "Tucker Maddock," he declared. "I never thought I'd be running into you at the Bi-Mart."

Tucker returned the smile and held out his hand to shake his former classmate's hand. "Good to see you, Neil."

Neil glanced down, his expression suddenly turning solemn. "I heard about Chris and his parents in that terrible car accident. I'm real sorry."

Tucker's throat tightened, and he fought back the emotion that threatened to consume him anew. "Yeah, me, too" was all he said.

As if sensing his discomfort in talking about his chosen family, Neil abruptly changed the subject. "You have a fine-looking family. I never considered you the marrying type." Then, turning to Ruth, he added, "You're a lucky lady. All during school, Tucker played by his own rules, but he always played fair."

"Actually, I'm not the marrying type," he admitted. At the look of surprise and pain that flashed across Ruth's face, Tucker was reminded of the time he'd overzealously tackled Chris in a game of backyard football. His friend had suffered a bruised rib, and Tucker had felt tremendously guilty for unintentionally hurting him. And although he didn't know why Ruth would be hurt by his casual comment, he still felt guilty for causing her pain. "This is my friend Ruth, her former student, Nicky and Nicky's sister, Angie.

Introductions were made all the way around, and Ruth and Evelyn seemed to hit it off.

"We're having a New Year's Eve party at our house," Evelyn told them. "I hope you both will come."

"Yeah, it'll be a blast," Neil chimed in. "Matt and Herbie and their wives are going to be there. They'd love to see you again."

Tucker bent and pressed his thumb against Nicky's toe as he'd seen Ruth and Evelyn do earlier. When he saw that there was plenty of growth room, he suggested he keep them on and wear them home. Then he turned back to his old friend. "I doubt I'll still be in Willow Glen at that time, but I appreciate your asking."

They said their good-byes and were at the front of the store before Ruth spoke.

"Cheer up," she told him as the kids each grabbed

a candy bar from the impulse-purchase rack in front of the cash register. "There are worse things than being mistaken for a married man."

Yes, there were worse things. Like losing your heart to a beautiful, sweet woman and two great little kids. Only to set yourself up for another terrible disappointment.

Tucker knew he should have been firmer about saying no to the Foutches' Christmas party. But when Aunt Shirley had brought him his freshly laundered clothes—clean and neatly folded—and started fussing over what he should wear that evening, she had thrown him off guard. And, when she saw that all he had brought with him was jeans, she'd fetched a pair of Uncle Oren's slacks for him to wear.

With her straightening his collar and adjusting the errant strand of hair over his left temple, she had reminded him of Mrs. Newland hovering over him on senior prom night, helping him to look his best for his date. He just didn't have the heart to say no.

The party was only three blocks away—well within walking distance during milder weather, but tonight they took Ruth's car. As she walked up the crowded driveway ahead of him and stepped gingerly onto the icy walk, her loose-fitting red silk skirt swished around her shapely legs. It reminded him of a sexy negligee, and the thought of her in bed stirred him despite the bitter night air. Tucker could have sworn he heard a dog howl, but quickly attributed it to his overheated libido.

Ruth stopped abruptly. "Did you hear that?"

Tucker collided with her, and his hands automatically went around her waist to prevent her from taking a tumble on the gray slate.

"Oiyuuuuuuuuuuuuu!"

"That?"

She nodded. His hands hadn't left her waist, and he made no attempt to remove them now. Her breath made a little cloud in front of her. Standing this close to her and feeling the narrowness of her slim hips through the bulky coat, he considered how she might react if he kissed her right now. The howl came again. This time, Tucker traced the sound to the Foutches' garage, where he suspected their dog had been impounded for the duration of the party.

"My thoughts exactly," he muttered.

"What?"

The front door opened, and the night was filled with Christmas music and the excited voices of partygoers. *"There* you are," said a small, middle-aged woman. She turned away from them for a moment to holler at someone in the house. "Hey, J.C., you can tell Aunt Shirley they're here."

When she turned back to them, she smiled warmly. "What with the patches of black ice on the roads, your aunt Shirley called to see if you made it here safely," she explained as they stepped inside.

Shrugging out of her coat, Ruth tilted her eyes heavenward. "My aunt is such a worrywart. When is she going to realize that I've grown up?"

If Aunt Shirley needed any evidence that her niece was, indeed, an adult, all she needed was to see her in this getup. Like the skirt, the top was loose and flowy, curving gracefully in all the right spots. The slick fabric did a fine job of showcasing her nipples, and Ruth crossed her arms self-consciously over her chest.

He blinked and looked again. He didn't know if he could withstand a whole evening of being close to her without touching her. The dog howled once more, only louder this time, and Tucker felt a strange urge to join in.

"So this is Cousin Tucker, the one I've heard so much about." Their hostess extended her hand to him. "I'm Tina Foutch. My husband, J.C., is over there mixing drinks. Just tell him your pleasure, and he'll get you whatever you want."

What he wanted didn't come from a bottle. Against his will, Tucker's gaze was drawn back to Ruth's bright red ensemble. He felt himself stiffen in response.

"There are a number of young women here who would love to make your acquaintance," Tina continued. "Why don't you introduce yourself around while I take your coats to the bedroom?" Then she snared Ruth's elbow. "Ruthie, you come with me. I want you to see the new curtains in our guest room."

About ten minutes later, Ruth rescued him from a bevy of brunettes, blondes and redheads. "You looked like you were in your element," she observed. "Sorry I broke up your crowd of admirers."

"I'd much rather talk to you," he said sincerely.

She tilted her head as if she wasn't sure whether to believe him. "Ever the charmer, you are."

"Just telling the truth." He took her hand in his. "You look beautiful tonight."

She shrugged, and the wide neckline slipped off one shoulder. Tucker let his eyes feast on the creamy smooth skin that enticed him to kiss her from earlobe to shoulder…and beyond.

"This isn't really my style," she said, hitching the fabric back into place. "Vivian insisted on lending it to me."

"Remind me to thank her later."

She blushed, and this time it was Tucker's turn to be charmed. Although she was less likely than some of the other women in the room to win a Miss Virginia contest, in his mind she was still the most beautiful.

The next hour went by in much the same fashion as most of these meet-greet-and-mingle parties went. Ruth introduced him to the parents of several of her students, a couple of friends from her own grammar school days, and the man she had dated briefly last year.

His name was Dillan, and Tucker instantly disliked him. For one thing, the guy kept looking at Ruth's chest, not that Tucker could blame him. But, still, it was the principle. For another, he smiled more than an insurance salesman. Tucker didn't trust anyone who smiled that much.

The clincher was when he kept trying to dredge up their mutual past with a bunch of "remember whens." Tucker was about to make a rude remark but was saved from shattering his reputation as a charmer when something brushed past his leg and shot into the dining room.

Tina followed a mere second later. "You come back here, Bitsy!"

Everyone watched, dumbfounded, as a small brown beagle launched itself from a chair onto the pedestal-leg dining table laden with biscuits, salads, gelatins, cookies, candy, chips and dip. Not to mention a chubby ceramic Santa who seemed more than a little amused by the latest turn of events.

But the real prize was the ham. For one gravity-defying instant, dog and table teetered like a spinning top about to run out of momentum. In the next instant, platters, laughing Santa and dog became airborne.

If the beagle were human, it could have won a football scholarship based solely on its midair tackle of the ham. The dog's legs were already churning when it hit the floor, and it managed to drag the ham—which rivaled it in size and weight—out of the dining area and into the living room.

Ruth was one of the first to break her spellbound disbelief and try to stop the food-snatcher, but the little dynamo eluded her. Others joined in, trying to run interference, but the animal dodged between their legs and darted around furniture, never once loosening its grip on the ham. And all the while, Tina was hollering, "Bitsy! Bitsy!"

Now the dog was running Tucker's way, its ears flapping in the self-made breeze. Tucker found himself admiring the mutt's persistence. If there was ever a time that he rooted for the underdog, it was now. A wide smile pulled at the corners of his mouth. It was all he could do to keep from egging her on with cheers of "Go, Bitsy!"

Until Dillan decided to be the hero. Pulling at his tie, Mr. Remember-When turned to Ruth—*Tucker's* date, for crying out loud—and announced that he would catch the dog.

Firing at a speed faster than light, Tucker's brain debated whether he should jump into the fray to save not only the ham but his chances with Ruth, as well. A bare second later, the little hound decided for him. Running between the two men as if daring them to catch it, the brown-and-black blur attempted to dive behind the glass-front china cabinet with its ill-gotten loot.

Dillan had bent down to try to snare the elusive beast when Tucker sailed in front of him, effectively blocking him and scoring the save for himself.

The dog let out a startled yelp when Tucker's arms closed around its squirming body. The china cabinet, which had received a glancing blow from Tucker's shoulder on his descent, teetered above him for a brief moment and then became still.

Breathing a sigh of relief, Tucker rose to his feet, clutching the panting dog to his chest.

"Bitsy! Oh, my poor Bitsy." Tina took the dog from him and accepted the grateful kisses it offered her.

Ruth moved to Tucker's side. "Are you all right?"

"Yeah, I'm fine, but I don't think the ham is going to survive."

She smiled. "At least you haven't lost your sense of humor." She brushed a bit of carpet fuzz from the front of his shirt. "It's a good thing Dillan had such fast reflexes. He grabbed the china cabinet just as it was about to fall on you."

He shot her a scorching frown and barely resisted the urge to test whether Dillan's reflexes were quick enough to dodge a fist in the nose.

Ruth chewed her lip and stared at him a full minute before speaking. "I don't know what your problem is tonight, but I hope you get over it real soon."

"I hope everyone has already eaten all the ham biscuits they wanted," Tina told the crowd of onlookers in an obvious attempt to lighten the mood. A murmur of chuckles ran through the room. "I'd like to apologize for Bitsy's atrocious behavior. She doesn't normally act like this, but she's been ravenous since she started nursing her puppies."

Nods of understanding came from some of the mothers in the room, and Ruth felt left out of the loop. One of her strongest wishes in life was to have children of her own. Babies to nurse and love and take care of. But most of all, she wanted a special man with whom to share those personal family experiences. Someone who would provide their children with a male role model and the guidance of a father who loved them...something she had missed growing up with her widowed Aunt Shirley.

For the first time, Ruth noticed the extent of the mess in the dining area. Food and broken pottery lay strewn on the floor. Fortunately, most of it was on the uncarpeted area. "I'll give J.C. a hand with that."

The other guests pitched in while Tina took Bitsy back to the garage. With so many helping hands, the task of cleaning up was accomplished in short order.

It wasn't long before the party started again in earnest. Tucker was refilling her glass when a man dressed in a Santa suit tapped Ruth's shoulder and asked what she wanted for Christmas.

She stared up into the familiar eyes and recognized the hazel irises she'd practically swooned over a year ago. They did nothing for her now as Dillan smiled down at her. The Santa outfit had nothing to do with his lack of appeal.

"I can't give you your heart's desire unless you tell me what you want," he persisted.

Her heart's desire. What she'd wished for all her life and wondered if she'd ever find it. A family. A real one, with a mother and a father and enough children—natural, foster or adopted, she didn't care—to fill a baseball team. Was that so much to ask for?

Ruth glanced back up at Dillan, who was waiting for her response. Maybe it was too much to ask. Maybe she should just be grateful that she'd had someone as loving and generous as Aunt Shirley to raise her and Vivian after their parents had died. And maybe she should be satisfied with the twenty-six children she taught—and mothered—every day of the school year.

Even so, this was Santa Claus she was talking to. She thought back to the year she had wanted an electric train set for Christmas. Embarrassed about asking for something her ultrafeminine older sister deemed a "boy's toy," she had kept quiet, hoping the jolly elf would intuitively know her wish and give her what she desired. She never got the train.

And now, in a superstitious attempt to avoid a replay of that disappointing Christmas, she stretched up and whispered into Santa's ear.

Music blared as someone put on a Christmas tape, and she felt the steadying pressure of Dillan's hand against her back as she wobbled on tiptoe. When she finished telling him her two long-held wishes and stepped away, he stared at her in amusement.

"Really?"

Ruth felt herself grow warm as she nodded a mute acknowledgment.

"Hey, I'm only Santa Claus," Dillan demurred with

a laugh. "I can help you with one of those wishes, but as for a family, you're on your own."

That was the problem. She was on her own.

Tucker returned from refilling their drinks, handed them both to her, and led Dillan almost forcibly to the other side of the room. Ruth started to follow them but, laden with the drinks, she had difficulty moving past the couples who danced to the music that someone had chosen on the stereo.

Helpless, she watched while the two men exchanged words. Dillan seemed intimidated in the face of Tucker's belligerence, and she couldn't help feeling sorry for her former boyfriend as he responded to the other man's questions.

Ruth sighed in exasperation. It was apparent Tucker didn't like Dillan—she didn't like him much herself—but she hoped he would be civil.

When Tucker returned a moment later, Dillan avoided her curious gaze and slunk off to another corner of the room. Tucker, on the other hand, seemed pleased with the outcome of their discussion.

He slipped a large, strong arm around her waist, and in the next moment Tucker was leading her to the center of the room where two other couples danced to the wistful strains of Bing Crosby's "White Christmas."

Ruth was taken aback when he took her hands in his and lifted them to his neck. Then he put his arms around her and began swaying to the music.

"It's customary for a gentleman to *ask* a lady to dance," she admonished, despite the cozy feeling that swept through her at his touch.

"It's also customary for a man to protect his date from an overly friendly ex-boyfriend."

"Why, 'Cousin' Tucker, if I didn't know better, I'd think you were jealous."

"Of *him?*" Tucker pulled her closer, and she enjoyed the feel of his chest. "I don't think so. I just don't like the guy."

She smiled up at him, wondering why and how he was stirring these emotions that made her head feel light. She'd only had one drink, but she decided to swear off alcohol for the rest of the night. It wouldn't do to release any more inhibitions on her baser instincts. "Well, if it makes you feel any better," she said, suddenly having an empathy for talk-show guests who felt the need to bare their ugliest secrets, "he dumped me for my sister."

"The fool."

She shrugged her shoulders to indicate her unconcern. Or maybe it was fatalism. "It's not like that was the first time it happened."

Though it had hurt at the time, in retrospect she saw her sister as something of a litmus test. Vivian had always been prettier and more outgoing than Ruth, whom the guys apparently thought paled in comparison. So when Vivian lowered her lashes or posed so that one curvy hip was thrust provocatively forward, men couldn't help but notice. Ruth didn't blame her sister for her dates' fickleness in choosing Vivian over her. After all, how could Ruth lose what was never hers? When the right man eventually came along, she told herself, he would see past Vivian's surface glitter. He would choose with his heart, not with his eyes. Or whatever.

Oddly, though, she hadn't felt as charitable when she had caught Vivian eyeing Tucker. She told herself it was because she was concerned with her sister's welfare. That she wanted to prevent the heartbreak that would inevitably come if Vivian became involved with the stranger who had insinuated himself into their midst. But a twinge of honesty forced her to admit that her feelings on the matter were more possessive than protective.

Ruth's neckline slid to one side, and before she could adjust the flimsy fabric on her shoulder, Tucker touched his lips to her skin. A melting sensation slid from her collarbone, where his mouth grazed, to the pit of her stomach and lower. This wasn't something that could be attributed to the single glass of wine she had sipped earlier.

When Tucker spoke, his voice was low and husky. "He'd have to be an idiot to choose her over you."

"Oh, get real." Ruth took a half step back, but his grip tightened around her waist and he pulled her closer. She'd gone this route before, and she knew the drill. "You've seen Vivian."

He gazed down at her, his eyes searching her face. Once again, she was being compared to her beautiful older sister. But this time it was different. This time the verdict seemed clearly in Ruth's favor.

"She's flashier, yes," Tucker admitted, "but you have substance."

Ruth sighed. "Substance. Isn't that sort of like telling the chubby girl she has a great personality?"

A smile tugged at the corner of his mouth. "If I were patronizing you, then why would I want to do this?"

As Bing crooned in the background, Tucker lowered his head and kissed her like she'd never been kissed before.

Ruth needed to get home, back in familiar surroundings, where she could regain her sense of perspective. Today had been too full of out-of-the-ordinary events, which led her thoughts to places they had no business lurking.

First there'd been the shopping spree with Tucker and the children. Even though they were only hers for a couple of days, she'd quickly fallen into the role of temporary mother, and Tucker's presence had made the pretend family seem complete. He'd played the part of father exceptionally well, except for that brief moment when his high school chum had mistaken him for a true family man.

Then, tonight at the party he'd been an attentive date, making her feel as though no other woman in the room existed. The gentle caring he'd shown her had made her longings increase even more. But she knew better than to let her emotions get wrapped up in this stranger who was almost certain to leave after he'd taken whatever he came back to Willow Glen Plantation to get.

She only hoped her heart would survive intact. But the longer he stayed, the more chance there was of being hurt. Already the brief glimpses of family and dating life had teased her into wanting much more. She wanted not only to see Tucker in his paternal and courting modes, but she also longed to discover what kind of lover he would be. An instinct of self-protection flared up in her soul, reminding her that she'd best stay away from that line of thought.

"Shirley left the parlor light on for us," Tucker said as they stepped into the house.

"As late as it is, I'm sure everyone's asleep." For some crazy reason, Ruth felt herself blush...as though he might be able to tie her mention of sleeping with her wayward thoughts of a moment ago.

She followed him into the parlor to turn off the lamp, only to be greeted by her very-much-awake Aunt Shirley.

Tucker chuckled softly. "Must be something about the women in this house...always waiting up for me to come home from my dates."

Shirley labored to pull herself upright on the couch. "I wish I could say that were so. Unfortunately, I didn't have much choice in the matter."

The older woman pulled a pained face, and Ruth was instantly alarmed. She rushed to her side, Tucker right behind her. "Aunt Shirley, what's the matter?"

"After I put the children to bed, I came in here to turn off the Christmas tree lights. My foot caught on that curl at the corner of the rug. Don't know what got into me, but I forgot all about that cussed thing. Next thing you know, I was in a heap on the floor." She rubbed her left hip. "It hurt too much to walk up to my bedroom, so I just parked my carcass right here."

"What about Boris and the others?" asked Ruth. "Why isn't one of them down here with you?"

"They were all asleep. I didn't want to risk waking up the children by shouting for someone. Besides, what could they have done that you two can't?"

"I'm sorry," said Tucker. "I should have fixed that carpet sooner."

Shirley made a steam sound with her lips. "Nonsense. You've already done too much."

Ruth squared her shoulders. Now was not the time for Tucker to be chalking up brownie points with her aunt. "We should get you to the hospital," she insisted. "You may have broken your hip."

"No, I think it's just bruised," she said, struggling to her feet. "Just help me up the stairs to my room. I'll be fine by breakfast."

"And if she's not, we'll take her to the hospital in the morning."

Tucker's interference was starting to get on her nerves. "But, Aunt Shirley—"

"Let her be." Tucker went to Shirley's side and put a helping arm around her plump waist. "We can put a cot in that little room under the stairs. And she'll be across the hall from the bathroom in case she needs to get up during the night."

Once again he was pushing his way in where he wasn't wanted. But she didn't dare argue with him because her aunt was so vulnerable right now. Then again, maybe that was why he was so insistent on helping.

Ruth gave herself a little shake. Maybe she should just go ahead and accept his help. Take him at face value and trust that he wouldn't hurt anyone in her family. After all, he hadn't given her any reason to distrust him.

Not yet, anyway.

She positioned herself on the other side of her aunt

to help steady her on the way to the tiny study that would be the older woman's bedroom for the night.

"Don't worry about me. Tucker won't let me fall." Shirley fanned her hand as if waving Ruth away. "Why don't you go unfold the cot? At the speed I'm going, you'll have it all set up by the time I get there."

Ruth had been usurped in her own house. She slanted her eyes at Tucker. To her annoyance, she found no sign of triumph in his expression. Only concern for her aunt.

Once they got Shirley settled in bed, Ruth stepped out into the hall where she could talk privately with Tucker. It was time for her to take back control of the situation. It wouldn't do to have their houseguest think he could call the shots around here.

"Thanks for your help," she said, sincerely grateful for the strong arms that had supported her aunt. "You can go up to bed now, and I'll sleep on the couch where I can listen out for her."

Tucker stopped her with a hand to her arm. Ruth tried not to think about the way he'd touched her when they'd been dancing. But the mere feel of his fingers gripping her in such an innocent way made her want more. Made her want him to hold her in a not-so-innocent way.

"You should sleep upstairs in case one of the kids needs you during the night." His gaze held hers. Even if he'd let go of her arm, she would have been unable to move. "It's a strange place for them. Angie, especially, would want a woman to comfort her if she gets scared or lonely during the night."

He was right. Although they'd taken to Tucker easily enough, she would feel better about taking care of them herself if either should need her. But what about Aunt Shirley? "I suppose I could ask Boris to come down here and stay with Shirley."

"That's not necessary," Tucker said with a firmness that brooked no argument. "I'll do it."

"Let the geezer sleep," Shirley called from her makeshift bedroom. "Besides, Cousin Tucker's strong muscles are better suited to the job."

Tucker smiled down at her and flexed his arm for her benefit. "She's right, you know."

"But—"

"If you don't stop arguing, I'll demonstrate by carrying you up those stairs to your room." His eyes smoldered with a fire that had started hours before at the party. "And I don't claim any responsibility for what might happen after I get you there."

Chapter Five

The nerve of him, saying something like that before she went to bed. His comment had affected her as strongly—maybe even more so—than that kiss under the holly. He had tapped into her secret yearning and played it like a fiddle. She supposed she ought to be extra careful, knowing that he might be merely setting her up.

But what if Aunt Shirley and the others were right about him? What if he really *was* being truthful about having spent part of his childhood in this house and leaving a blood-brothers' pact in the attic? Ruth could feel her defenses slipping as her motives for wanting to know more about him changed. She'd started out wanting the information so she could better protect her family. And now she wanted to know him better for purely personal reasons.

And those personal thoughts kept her from drifting off to a peaceful sleep. By the time she awoke the next morning, the feeble winter sun had already been up for a while.

Slipping out from under the toasty comforter, Ruth quickly changed into a warm sweater to ward off the room's chill. Children's voices rang out in the side yard, and she stepped over to the window to watch Nicky and Angie in a game of tag. Uncle Oren was out there with them, wrapping his arms around his thin frame. The children were using him as "basc."

Ruth laughed to think how easily the kids had seen through the older man's gruff exterior. But even though he was being a good sport about their antics, he shouldn't stay very long in the cold. Grateful to her uncle for entertaining them so she could sleep through the children's rising and breakfast, she hurried to finish dressing and go downstairs to relieve him. But first she would check on Aunt Shirley to see how her hip had fared through the night.

She opened her door to the hall and sat on the bed to finish tying her shoes. A deep male voice came from Tucker's room. From the sound of it, he was on his personal phone, conducting business.

"If you can handle the Birchmont case without me, then I'll plan on staying in Willow Glen at least through Christmas."

A window opened downstairs, and Aunt Shirley called out to Nicky to put his stocking cap back on. Ruth felt herself relax, knowing that if Aunt Shirley was up and policing the children then she must be feeling better than she did last night.

"Yeah, an opportunity has just presented itself, and I'd be a fool not to take advantage of it. So I'll be here until the deal is closed." Tucker sighed heavily.

"The banks are incredibly slow about processing paperwork during the holidays, but I think I can hurry things along by juggling some accounts."

Ruth's chest squeezed until she thought she might pass out. Although she'd finished tying her shoelaces, she stayed where she was, resting her cheek against her knees until her pulse steadied.

First there was the roofing repair swindle. Then along came a so-called financial counselor who'd advised her gullible aunt to buy into an unsecured investment deal. And now Tucker had an "opportunity" that involved arrangements with the bank. And, most likely, her aunt.

She took a deep breath. On the other hand, maybe it wasn't as bad as she thought. Perhaps it was her foolish hope that this was all a misunderstanding that had her searching for another explanation. Considering how sweet he'd been to her, the kids and her aunt, she owed him the benefit of the doubt. After all, he hadn't actually said the deal involved Aunt Shirley. It was entirely possible that he had legitimate business connections that he was handling by phone.

His voice came to her clearly now as she pondered what she'd just overheard.

"Can you overnight something to Willow Glen before Christmas? It's really important."

He lowered his voice, and all Ruth could hear was deep murmuring. Considering how thin the walls in this old house were, it would be an easy matter to hear the rest of his conversation by pressing her ear to the wall. But, as Aunt Shirley had drummed into her while she was growing up, two wrongs did not make a right.

Still, giving him the benefit of the doubt did not

mean burying her head in the sand. Prudence called for her to keep a close watch on Tucker Maddock. She would do whatever it took to protect her aunt, even if it meant sticking by his side twenty-four hours a day.

Ruth's foot had fallen asleep, but she didn't have the heart to ask little Angie to move. Overwhelmed by her new situation, the little girl occasionally hid behind her brother or clung to Ruth when she needed to retreat. Angie's thumb had seldom come out of her mouth since she arrived here, and after this morning's game of tag she sat on Ruth's foot and wrapped her arms around her leg.

In an effort to encourage blood circulation, Ruth wiggled her toes inside her shoe. Angie giggled. It was a bubbly sound that Ruth knew she could never tire of.

"Come on," she said, putting aside the book she'd been reading. "We need to make sure Aunt Shirley's not overdoing it with her hip." Although Ruth and most of the other members of the house had offered to cook dinner, Aunt Shirley had insisted that she was fully recovered from last night's fall. And she'd insisted on preparing the meal without any help from "hovering worrywarts."

She walked the child, still balancing on Ruth's foot, into the kitchen, where Tucker and Nicky had just come in from outside after tinkering under the hood of Tucker's car. Dishes clattered in the dining room, and Ruth deduced that Aunt Shirley was setting the table.

Another giggle burst loose from Angie as Ruth made her way through the room with a stiff-legged shuffle. Tucker caught her eye, and they shared a moment of connection that Ruth had never experienced before. It was as though their hearts shared the same thoughts. They were bound by a warmth that defied the wintry day…a feeling of familial togetherness that, while including the children, was at the same time exclusive to the two of them alone. No words were spoken, but that one look had said everything she ever wanted to hear.

Goodness, how she loved having children in the house. She didn't dare consider how she felt about having Tucker here to share the experience. Especially not after that conversation she'd overheard this morning.

A few minutes later, after the children had rung the decorative dinner bell by the front desk, the gang swarmed to the dining room. A couple of the men had brought in an extra table and pushed it next to the big one to make room for the children. Tucker and Dewey sat beside each other, enjoying a joke as the others piled into their assigned seats.

The two men laughed at something only they understood, and Ruth assumed it had something to do with the jokes they'd told each other over the past few days. Oddly, Ruth felt left out, and she didn't like feeling this way. Although she told herself it was because she wanted to be aware of Tucker's interactions in order to protect her family, the discomfort went deeper.

She didn't like being left out of their inside joke, and she didn't like that she wanted to be closer to the center of Tucker Maddock's attention.

Despite her initial assessment of him, she'd since

come to learn that he was a caring and giving person. It wasn't only the clothes he bought for the children that made her think so. Or the fact that he'd been so concerned about her aunt's well-being after her fall. He was thoughtful in other, more subtle ways as well.

She didn't know why Tucker occupied her thoughts so much. Didn't know why she was so inescapably attracted to him. Especially since he'd said flat out that he wasn't the marrying type. So why was she wasting her energy and longing on him when what she wanted was a solid, reliable man to marry? When she wanted someone who would give her the children she wanted so desperately and help her raise them? When she wanted someone that she felt certain was decent and honest and trustworthy?

Tucker was the exact opposite of the kind of man she was looking for. He drove a two-seater car. He had no family, nor did he seem to want one. And no matter how many times he showed himself to be a kind and caring person, she couldn't help wondering if that was only part of his act...an act designed to reap whatever rewards he sought. The only thing they had in common was that he, too, was searching for something. But though Ruth knew what she wanted from life, Tucker seemed to be drifting in his search.

Begrudgingly, she admitted to herself that Vivian, with her lack of commitment and fickle attitude toward men, was probably better suited to Tucker. Ruth sighed. Judging by the way the two had tarried together in the hallway yesterday, she supposed they'd already figured that out.

Aunt Shirley set a bowl of steaming vegetables on the table and took her place at the end. "Tucker and

I had a nice long chat last night after you went to bed," she said to Ruth. "That man is full of interesting ideas."

From the corner of her eye, Ruth caught him giving her aunt a small shake of the head, as if to stop her from saying more.

Curious, Ruth started to probe for details, but was interrupted when Nicky tried to reach for the salt shaker, which resulted in a short etiquette lesson from Aunt Shirley.

"Would you pass the salt, please?" the boy asked Tucker.

Tucker grinned. "Overhand or underhand?"

Instead of being affronted that her houseguest had wreaked havoc on her attempt at teaching the children manners, Aunt Shirley gave Tucker an indulgent smile. It looked like Ruth's wasn't the only heart he'd won over.

Aunt Ada seemed to have come out of a daydream she'd been having. "What a pretty pink shirt you're wearing," she told the younger child.

Angie got up on her knees and arched her back so everyone could see the pattern of purple elephants marching across the bottom of her knit top. "Cousin Tucker bought it for me. It matches my new shoes. See?"

"Angie, don't put your feet on the table," Nicky scolded.

She put her foot back in her chair and proceeded to announce, "Miss Marsh and Cousin Tucker are gonna be my new mama and daddy."

Ruth practically toppled her glass of iced tea. "What?"

"Close your mouth, Cousin Tucker," said Aunt Shirley, "before you swallow a fly."

"That's stupid," Nicky said in response to his sister's comment. "What makes you think they're going to be our parents?"

"The man in the store said so."

Tucker cleared his throat. "The man in the store was a friend of mine that I haven't seen in a long time," he explained to Angie, as well as to the rest of the openmouthed family. "He made a mistake when he thought you two were my children."

Angie's mouth formed a silent "Oh." In an afterthought, she giggled. "That's silly. We got different daddies. That's why Nicky has black hair and I got yellow."

"Shut up," said Nicky.

Angie whirled in her seat to face her brother. "I didn't tell 'em that your daddy's a deadbeat."

Despite his olive complexion, Nicky reddened. "You'd better quit listening in on Mom's phone conversations." To cover his embarrassment as he became aware of the rest of the family taking in their exchange, he said simply, "She's my half sister."

That had been obvious from the first time any of them had laid eyes on the children. In contrast to Nicky's Mediterranean darkness, Angie was blond and pink-skinned. Their common feature, large hazel-green eyes, served to enhance and contrast the children's individual good looks. Ruth supposed that once Angie lost the baby fat that gave her face a cherubic roundness, she and Nicky would look more like brother and sister.

The rest of the family nodded and smiled at the

boy's statement and dug into their dinner. Ruth picked up her fork and noticed that Tucker sat silently, the hand holding his tea glass suspended between the table and his mouth as he studied the children. On anyone else, the drawing together of his eyebrows and the thinning of his lips as his observant eyes roamed their little faces could have seemed like a judgment of some sort. But to Ruth it seemed clear that the man beside her had questions. And concern. And pain.

Mostly pain.

As his heart so obviously went out to the children, her heart also went out to him.

She allowed herself to study him as he'd done Nicky and Angie, except that she examined him via her peripheral vision and quick glances. His perusal of the children finally broken, he lifted the glass to his mouth and drank. Ruth found herself strangely fascinated by the movement of his Adam's apple along his wide neck.

She wondered what he had looked like as a boy. With his dark coloring similar to Nicky's, she supposed he may have resembled her former student. Had he been a quiet child, or loud and rambunctious? Serious or playful? He certainly seemed sentimental about the Newland family. She thought it odd that, although he'd spoken of the Newlands on several occasions, he had not once mentioned his own family.

She didn't know what ghosts haunted the stranger who had recently joined their family. All she knew was that she wanted once again to see the charming smile he wore so well.

He turned back to Nicky. "So she's your half sister, huh?"

Nicky nodded and pushed his hair back in imitation of the gesture he'd previously seen Tucker use.

"Which half?"

"Huh?"

"Is she divided left and right, top and bottom or front and back?"

"I don't know."

"Seems to me you ought to find out so you'll know which half of her to treat like a sister."

Tucker separated the peas from the carrots on his plate and then mixed them back together again. He felt Ruth's eyes on him. It was anyone's guess why the kids had brought the subject up, but he couldn't let it drop now. It was too important to ignore.

Ruth made herself busy refilling her tea glass and getting up to get more ice. She seemed intent on hearing about Brooke's latest crush as the teen steered her end of the table to a subject closer to her own interests. Even so, Tucker knew Ruth was listening to what he had to say to Nicky.

"I didn't have a brother or sister," he began. "Not a stepbrother or half sister. But there was a special friend that I'll always think of as part of my family. Chris and his parents were closer to me than my blood relatives."

"Did Chris ever get on your nerves?" the boy asked with a pointed glance at Angie.

"Plenty of times, but I got on his nerves sometimes, too."

How could he explain to Nicky that he shouldn't measure or weigh the wonderful kinship he had with his sister? That he should just enjoy it and claim their common bond without condition? Would the boy have to grow up some more before he fully understood?

"Family isn't about how much of the same blood you share. Family is how you feel here," he said, placing a hand over his heart.

Then, to dispel the incredibly sappy feeling that seemed to cling to the words he'd just spoken, he wadded his napkin and tossed it at the boy.

Tucker rolled a towel and laid it over the ridge where the bedroom window locked. Some things never changed. Like the draftiness of this old house.

And the way he'd been sucked back into the family in this house. They were a terrific group of people— all of them. He wondered if the house was a magnet for people like the Newlands. And for him.

Turning away from the window and the view of the carriage house out back, he kicked off his shoes and sat on the bed to pull off his socks. This house had always been a haven for him in the past, and he'd expected that merely being here would bring back that sense of security he'd always known here.

But how could he feel safe and secure when being among Ruth's family intensified all that Tucker had ever treasured…and lost?

He dropped his socks in a heap on the floor and wished he could shuck his cares so easily. Unfortunately, his cares extended to Ruth, her family and now the two kids who had wormed their way into the house and his heart.

This Christmas was certainly not going the way he'd planned. So maybe he should take a step back and return to the original plan…to be in the house and soak up the memories that lingered here, while avoiding all the pain and hoopla of celebrating Christmas. To do so would mean spending a good portion of his time here in this room. It would also require that he avoid creating any more new memories with the family that had all but adopted him as their own. He'd have to think of something to get this situation back to a bed-and-breakfast arrangement. Meanwhile, first thing tomorrow, he would go shopping for a television, VCR and a supply of eggnog to keep him company while he lost himself in action videos.

A tap at the door stopped him before he removed his shirt. Walking to the door, he shivered as his bare feet left the braid rug and touched the hardwood floor.

It was Ruth, the only woman he knew who could manage to look sexy in a sweatshirt. Suddenly he was no longer aware of the cold in the room. To distract himself, he tried to focus on the prissy flowers on her collar that gave her an appearance of innocence. Even so, he felt himself snap to attention.

"If you came to tuck me in," he said before thinking, "you're just in time."

She gave him a look that he supposed she used on her students. It was pretty good. If he were ten years old again, he'd be intimidated.

"I'll give you an A for effort," she told him, "but an F for failing to realize that the only hooker in this house is Aunt Ada."

Tucker laughed and opened the door wider. He was rewarded when her eyes softened and she smiled in return. He offered her a chair, but she refused it. "What can I do for you?"

Ruth allowed her gaze to sweep the room. Except

for a towel in the window and socks on the floor, their guest was quite neat. "I don't know what you do for a living, but if you ever decide to change occupations, you should consider becoming a teacher."

The startled expression he wore told her his mind was still on his invitation. Come to think of it, once the thought snagged her mind, it refused to let go…just as the memory of their kisses had popped up time and again. If he'd wanted to drive her crazy, he could have found no better way to taunt and torment her. Except, maybe, with the image of him in bed, waiting to be tucked in. Irrationally, she wondered if he slept naked.

But that wasn't why she had come to his room tonight. *Stay on task, Ruth,* she urged herself, much the same as she would remind her easily distracted students.

"You have a way with children," she added as explanation. "Nicky and Angie have really taken to you. In fact they've already asked if you'll take them for a ride in your car."

A wariness flickered across his handsome features. Like those morphing cartoon characters that the boys in her class often talked about, Tucker shed his smiling persona and assumed the characteristics of a totally different man. His eyes expressionless and the curve of his mouth hard and straight, he shut her out as effectively as if he'd closed the door in her face.

Well, she could be cool, too. "Anyway, Angie insisted on taking her string to bed with her so she could practice the cat's cradle you taught her. I thought it was sweet the way you were trying to help her break her thumb-sucking habit."

It *was* sweet. Not just the fact that he was helping her, but the way he helped her. When he'd jokingly asked Angie if he could "have some of that," the little girl had been certain he was going to tease her like the kids at school did. Instead, Tucker had admitted that he, too, had sucked his thumb when he was young. He had stopped, he told Angie, when he didn't need it anymore.

And then he had taught her to fashion a cat's cradle out of an old shoelace so she would have something to do in place of sucking her thumb.

"It's not something for her to be ashamed of," he said as if daring Ruth to disagree. "I was only trying to distract her because her thumb was so chapped."

And that was another reason she'd been so charmed by what he did. Not once did he chastise the girl for seeking the comfort she so obviously needed. Instead, he'd focused on the need to allow her skin to heal.

Ruth nodded. "I put some petroleum jelly on it and covered it with a bandage."

Tucker morphed again as he offered her another of the warm smiles that made her knees feel as mushy as the ointment she'd used on Angie. "Very clever. If she doesn't rip it off during the night, the bandage ought to slow her down."

She was pleased by his approval. She found herself wanting to prolong the sensation, but didn't know quite how. Instead, she blathered the first thing that came to mind. "It would mean a lot to Angie and Nicky if you popped in to tell them good night. Even though they seem to be adjusting well to staying with us, they still miss their parents."

It felt so odd, and so good at the same time, to be

discussing the children with Tucker. She was glad he'd been there when Nicky and Angie needed them. He had helped her immensely, not only in entertaining the children, but in allowing her to lean on him. She supposed she could have muddled through by herself, just as she'd done the couple of times she'd taken in foster children. But it wouldn't have been the same.

This time it seemed as though the children and she and Tucker were all connected by invisible bonds. They were joined in a way that four strangers could not be. It was as if they were...*family*.

No wonder Neil and Evelyn had thought they were married. They must have noticed the connection that she and Tucker felt for each other and the kids.

She stood in front of him, dazed at the realization, and studied him as carefully as if she were shopping for a father for her own children.

Besides being tall, handsome and big-muscled—traits she noticed the first time she saw him—he was also a bit rough and dangerous-looking. Depending on how he dressed, he looked as though he would be equally comfortable fending for himself in a barroom brawl or intimidating high-powered businessmen in a corporate boardroom.

She'd already seen glimpses of his sentimentality as well as his obvious concern for the children. When he watched a football game, he probably cheered for the underdog team. Though she barely knew him and the phone conversation she overheard this morning tempted her to believe otherwise, she was convinced he was a man of strong character. A man of his word. A man who, when he decided to give of himself, did so completely.

Those certainly were traits she'd look for in the man who would be the father of her children someday. As for mate qualities, there was no doubt that he tempted her on an emotional and physical level. He intrigued her, making her wonder which she wanted more—to probe his mind or explore his body.

Ruth realized her perusal had drawn her attention to one area of his body that particularly intrigued her. She pulled her gaze back to his face to find him studying her as critically as she'd examined him. With a wicked and horrified fascination, she wondered if he had somehow read her thoughts and responded accordingly. The thought pleased her, and she felt a small smile tug at the corner of her lips.

Lifting his arms, he ran his fingers through his hair, pausing to press the heels of his hands against his temples. He closed his eyes and exhaled loudly. When he opened his eyes again, he fixed them on Ruth, and she quivered with a delight that she could not name.

"I have a lot of paperwork to do tomorrow," he said abruptly. "I'll say good night to the kids, but I won't be available to spend a lot of time with them like I did today."

At the questioning look she threw him, he turned away and strode to the bureau. His back to her, he opened a drawer and paused. Then, as if dismissing her not only from his room, but from his life, he added, "I'm sure you'll manage fine on your own."

Chapter Six

It was the morning before Christmas Eve. Ruth sat cross-legged on the parlor floor with Nicky and Angie, helping them make Christmas ornaments from pictures cut out of magazines.

Her aunts, uncles and cousins were busy shopping, wrapping last-minute gifts or otherwise keeping a low profile. Aunt Ada had stayed locked in her room all morning with a stash of colored yarns and canvas. She'd been very hush-hush about a special project she was working on, and Ruth had decided to follow her lead and get the kids involved in a craft of their own.

The Johnsons would be returning today to pick up Nicky and Angie. And Ruth would once again face a house without children in it. The emptiness would be difficult to bear, but she would manage.

On her own.

The separation this time would be harder than the two times Ruth had cared for foster children. The first had been for a month during her summer break while a child's parent served a misdemeanor jail sentence. The other had been an overnight emergency stay while Social Services found room for two girls and their mother at a women's shelter. On both occasions, Ruth had carefully guarded her heart as she sought to make her guests comfortable during their difficult time.

But with Nicky and Angie it was different. This time she'd had Tucker to help her watch the children and share the fun times.

But Tucker had made it clear he had no desire to continue those special moments. He didn't have to slam a door in her face for her to take the hint. Tucker had made it quite clear that his agenda—whatever that might be—did not include children.

She hadn't seen him all morning, which led her to assume that, like Aunt Ada, he had sought privacy in his room. In a few minutes, she would take a break from making paper ornaments and make sure he wasn't snooping in the attic again. At least, that was the reason she gave herself for wanting to go in search of him.

Nicky set down the last in a stack of magazines and shared a look of annoyance.

"What are you looking for, Nicky?"

"I wanted a picture of a dog, but the only one I found had a stupid bow on top of his head."

Ruth held back a smile. Nicky much preferred roughhousing and outdoor sports to cutting, pasting and tying ribbons. But, since she had encouraged the children to wait to play outside until the midday sun nudged the thermostat upward, she'd best do what she could to keep him entertained until then.

"Mama said we can get a dog someday," Angie declared, "when we get a house with a yard."

Ruth impulsively hugged the child. Their parents were struggling so hard to give them what they needed. A luxury such as a puppy would have to wait until other, more pressing matters were taken care of.

"I hope that 'someday' comes very soon." Rising to her feet, she turned and laid a hand on Nicky's shoulder. "I saw Uncle Oren carrying some of his old firefighting magazines to the recycle pile. Maybe one of them has a picture of a Dalmatian in it."

She had him help his sister punch a hole in the top of her ornament while she went to look for the magazines.

As Ruth entered the empty kitchen, she thought she heard her sister's voice coming from the jalousied porch at the side of the house. Preparing herself for the cold from the poorly insulated room, she opened the door and stepped into the midst of an obviously private chat.

Tucker and Vivian, seated on the wicker loveseat with their heads bowed closely together, were so engaged in their conversation that at first they appeared not to hear Ruth come in. Their attention was focused on a sheet of paper that Tucker held, and Vivian's hand rested ever-so-casually on his knee, as if she were bracing herself for a better look. He seemed unaware of her touch as he smiled into those enormous pale-blue eyes of hers.

But Ruth knew better than to think this was just an innocent discussion between two casual acquaintances. It had happened so many times before that the lump of foreboding wedging itself in her stomach was easy to identify. Va-Va-Vivian was at it again. The Vampire Vixen was going in for the kill.

It shouldn't bother her. Not this time, and certainly not with this man.

She told herself her reaction was more protective than possessive. After all, his earnest gaze seemed to be seeking something from her sister. Both had stopped talking, and he was waiting for an answer. Or something else.

Sickened to think that she had stumbled upon a couple about to share more than just conversation, Ruth thought she might cry out in pain as Tucker leaned closer to her sister. She herself had tasted his kisses…even dreamed about them, and it broke her heart to think that he could so casually share them with someone else. First Tucker had moved in on her family, and now it seemed he was moving in on Vivian.

Ruth cleared her throat. "I'm sorry, I didn't know anyone was in here." That wasn't totally true. She'd known someone was here, but she hadn't realized they were in the middle of such a private exchange.

The pair jumped apart as if caught in the act of wrongdoing. Rising to his feet, Tucker smoothly slid the paper behind him. Vivian snagged it and wordlessly tucked it into her purse before lining up beside him…poised as though before a firing squad.

He pretended to ignore what Vivian had done and instead seemed only to have eyes for Ruth. *My, how easily he turned the charm off and on.*

"No problem," he said. "We were just finishing up our discussion."

"Indeed." She didn't bother to mask her skepticism.

The purse pinned under her arm, Vivian pulled her jacket together and zipped it up. Either she had already been on her way out, or she had planned to linger with Tucker on the barely heated porch for a while. Ruth suspected the latter.

At least Vivian had the grace to act sheepish. ''I, uh, need to run to the bank before it closes for the holiday. While I'm out, do you want me to pick up anything for you?''

At first Ruth thought it was her imagination, but a disconcerting observation became obvious as Vivian edged toward the outside door. Her sister would not look her in the eye. Ruth felt a disappointment that sank to the pit of her soul and colored her emotions a depressing shade of gray. ''No, thanks. I'm sure you picked up all you can handle for today.''

Vivian slanted her eyes in Ruth's direction but didn't respond. A moment later, she was backing her little red car out of the driveway.

Unable to speak, Ruth moved past Tucker and started pulling magazines out of the wicker hamper where the recyclable paper was stored. She really wasn't that surprised by her sister's behavior. Vivian had, after all, set a precedent by unburdening her of previous beaus, the most recent one being Dillan. This latest episode was all a part of the pattern.

What surprised her was how easily Tucker had fallen into Vivian's trap. Yet she shouldn't have been surprised by his behavior. Tucker Maddock was a stranger in the family...an unwanted stranger whose motives for being here were not entirely clear. And then there'd been that time when he and Vivian had dawdled upstairs and Tucker had returned with lipstick on his face. Ruth had preferred to think it was her own shade, or even that her affectionate aunt had left the mark on him, but now it was painfully clear that she'd been deluding herself.

Pushing past the newspapers, she dug up more magazines from the bottom of the basket and stacked them on her arm. She supposed she shouldn't blame Tucker for falling prey to her sister's predatorial tactics. He was only a man…a man with eyes and hormonal urges.

But, against her better judgment, Ruth had believed deep down that he was different from the rest. She'd thought him somehow wiser and…well, above falling for a woman merely because she had wicked blue eyes and a pretty pair of legs.

''Can I give you a hand with that?''

Too late, Ruth realized she'd been showing her peevishness by haphazardly scattering papers on the floor.

Tucker bent to retrieve them, and his arm grazed hers. Ruth stiffened against his touch…against the possibility that she might once again notice the warmth and strength in his arms and start wishing he would wrap them around her.

''No, thank you,'' she murmured. ''You've done enough already.''

Kneeling beside her, Tucker stilled her jerky movements with a hand to her wrist. Ruth stopped what she was doing and stared down at the big fingers that rested on the small area of skin left bare by her three-quarter-length sleeve. Suddenly she became overwhelmingly aware of the chill in the room. Of the cold that had seeped into her heart.

''It's not what you think,'' he said.

His voice was warm, and she longed to seek refuge in his words. The next few seconds hung like limp laundry between them as she waited for him to explain what he meant, and she imagined that he would clear away her doubts and dismay with a logical, reasonable explanation. But he didn't say what her foolish heart wanted to hear.

"You need to trust me. That's all I ask."

He made it sound so simple. Maybe that was the problem. Maybe he thought *she* was simple.

"That's not so easy for me to do, *Cousin* Tucker." She shifted the magazines to her other arm. "Less than a week ago, a stranger dropped into our house. Since then, he has been methodically working each member of the family. Can you tell me why I should trust someone like that?"

His hand hadn't moved from her arm, and her resolve threatened to weaken.

"Just give me time. Then you'll understand." He pulled away and put his hand over his heart. "I promise."

Ruth moved toward the kitchen, unwilling to hear more of the platitudes that she wanted to believe, but which logic told her were false. She didn't need more time to understand that in these few short days he'd invaded her soul and ransacked her hopes and dreams.

"I've already given you more than I should have." Namely, her heart.

Tucker had considered skipping lunch to take full advantage of his self-imposed isolation. If he were honest with himself, he'd admit that he didn't want to face Ruth after the way he'd brushed her off last night. And after what had taken place this morning.

It had required enormous restraint not to take her in his arms after he saw the crushed look on her face. The look *he* had put there. Guilt still twisted in his gut, a sensation that he told himself was only hunger pangs. He went downstairs to join the rest of the family for their midday meal.

Greetings were given all around. Ruth also murmured a hello and promptly turned away from him to help Angie hold her fork properly. Tucker didn't blame her for not speaking to him.

Even so, he didn't regret his action. In fact, it was kinder to let her know—and remind himself—that any attraction between them would only lead to a dead end. Not that he flattered himself to think she was interested in him. It was just that any man with two eyes could see that she was a woman ripe for marriage. Every time she looked at one of the children, it was obvious she wanted a family of her own. She wanted permanence and commitment, something that Tucker could have no part.

Sure, family and commitment were great things to have, he admitted. But when he considered how much it hurt to lose them—and he always did—it seemed safer not to get involved in the first place. He had learned long ago that there was no such thing as permanence. So why torture himself?

As for Ruth, it seemed wiser to remove himself from the running before she decided to put him on her list of possible mates.

The same went for the kids. Angie had clung to him last night when he kissed her, and Nicky had tried to delay his leaving the room after he tucked the boy in. It was kinder for everyone, Tucker knew, to avoid an attachment now that would be painful to sever later.

He ate half his lunch and decided he wasn't so hungry after all. Aware that Ruth was watching him as if he were a fox pacing around the chick coop, he flashed her a conciliatory smile. "Relax and enjoy your meal," he told her. "I'm not going to touch your radishes."

Ruth inhaled sharply and choked on her salad. Tucker turned to help her, but Uncle Oren had already jumped up and dashed around the table to whack her on the back.

"Cousin Tucker," Angie cried, "don't let him hurt Miss Ruth!"

Aunt Ada tried to reassure the girl. "It's okay. Oren's a retired firefighter. He has emergency medical training."

By now, Tucker was kneeling beside Ruth, holding her hand as she tried to catch her breath. Although her face had turned Christmas red and her eyes watered from coughing, she was taking in air. He put up a hand to stop Oren's pounding on her back. "She'll be all right. Just let her cough for a moment."

When the older man didn't immediately stop, Angie jumped down from her chair and kicked him in the ankle. Oren promptly ceased his lifesaving efforts and started hopping up and down on one foot while holding the other in his hand. He didn't move like a man who needed a cane.

"What did she do that for?" Dewey demanded.

Angie was almost as red-faced and every bit as

teary-eyed as the woman she sought to protect. "He was hitting Mama Ruth," she sobbed.

By now, Ruth's coughing had subsided, and she honked into the paper napkin Tucker handed her. When she had composed herself, she turned a cow-eyed look on the little girl. "What did you call me, sweetheart?"

Angie took a step back, as if she were afraid of being scolded for her slip of the tongue. "I'm sorry. I meant 'Miss' Ruth."

Ruth leaned forward and swept the child into her arms. "That's okay. I didn't mind."

Tucker watched the exchange with trepidation. It was obvious the little girl had innocently pushed Ruth's "family" button.

Nicky met Tucker's eyes. "Girls," he declared.

Tucker responded with a rolling of the eyes.

Aunt Ada ceased patting Oren's shoulder and rose from the table. Looking pointedly at Tucker, she said, "You come with me. I have a surprise to show you."

Tucker frowned as the tiny, round woman waddled from the room. The rest of the family, beaming high-wattage smiles at him, urged him to follow their aunt. Cautiously, as if the woman might be waiting to ambush him, Tucker entered the parlor.

She stood by the fireplace where a row of brightly colored Christmas stockings adorned the mantel. In her hand she held an oversize stocking with the image of a poinsettia sewn onto it. Above the red flower were two words carefully and lovingly stitched in white yarn. *Cousin Tucker.*

"I wanna see the surprise," Angie said, bouncing

up and down beside him. The rest of the family had followed them and were waiting for his reaction.

"I'm not just a hooker," Aunt Ada declared proudly. "I'm a needlepointer, too!"

Tucker tried to take a breath, but it seemed as though the atmosphere had been sucked out of the room. His pulse pounded in his ears.

"I hope you don't mind that I put *Cousin* on it," Aunt Ada continued, apparently unaware that Tucker was threatening to hyperventilate, "but it wouldn't have sounded right if it said *Nephew* Tucker."

She handed the stocking to him and waited. Tucker knew she was waiting for a compliment or—at the very least—a thank you.

When none was immediately forthcoming, she turned back the top to expose the fabric inside. "It's lined, too."

It was obvious that, no matter how firm his intentions to lock himself away in his room—avoiding not only Christmas but the family as well—he wouldn't be able to isolate himself. He could pretend that his relationship with this family was that of a boarder at a bed-and-breakfast inn, but there was no mistaking that he had been accepted as a member of the clan. They had adopted him, with or without his consent.

"You really shouldn't have" was all he could manage to say.

Aunt Ada pressed the stocking into his hand, the meaning behind her gesture obvious: by accepting the stocking, he would also be accepting his new position in the family.

The nubby fabric chafed him, seemingly burning a

brand into his skin. Tucker felt as though he was suffocating.

Angie pulled the stocking from his hand to ooh and aah over it. Releasing his hold on the scrap of fabric that represented more than just a means of holding candy and trinkets, he finally managed to suck in a deep breath of air. When he did so, his head felt light, as if he might pass out. He mumbled a thank-you and rushed from the room.

He needed space. Rushing through the kitchen and out onto the jalousied porch, he didn't stop until he stepped outside into the frigid December afternoon. The cold air served to snap him from his stupor. A gust of wind swept over him, crawling under his flannel shirt and forcing his muscles to contract against the onslaught.

Behind him, he heard the family filing out onto the porch. He took another deep breath and felt the icy air sting his sinuses, reminding him of the ice-cream headaches he got as a kid. Good. The physical pain distracted him from the other stuff going on inside him.

He heard Uncle Oren's voice first. "Leave the boy alone, Shirley. Can't you see he's all choked up?"

Aunt Shirley ignored her brother-in-law, as usual. "Young man, come in here before you catch your death of cold." Addressing those around her, she added, "He's not even wearing a coat."

Ruth stood beside Aunt Ada in the kitchen as they watched the rest of her family mill around on the porch.

Ada looped her hand through the crook of Ruth's arm. "Do you think he really liked my stocking that much?"

Ruth smiled and patted her aunt's knobby fingers.

"Most men wouldn't want you to know how sentimental they are," Ada continued in a hushed voice as if divulging a secret. "He must be in touch with his feminine side."

"I doubt that," Vivian said, coming up behind them. "Every side I've seen is definitely masculine."

Trying not to cringe at her sister's words, Ruth distracted herself by straightening the collar of Aunt Ada's cardigan. Vivian left no doubt that her head had been turned by the stranger in their house. Ruth was certain the other woman wouldn't let up until she had him in her clutches.

"If you think he's hot," Brooke said, "you should see the new guy on my favorite soap opera. Wanna go watch?"

Vivian snorted. "Not me. I'm going shopping."

"Can I go with you?"

After the way they'd been bickering the past several days, Ruth expected Vivian to reject their cousin's request with a scathing comment. When she said yes, Ruth reasoned that she'd been overcome with Christmas cheer.

"Sure, but only if you stop telling people I'm your mother."

They left the room together, chatting about the bargains they hoped to find. But Ruth was more interested in what was happening out back.

Tucker had wandered out to the carriage house.

Bored by the lack of excitement, the aunts, uncles, cousins and children filed back into the house.

"He's out there messing with his car," Aunt Shirley

told her. "You should go talk some sense into his head. He wouldn't listen to me."

Angie raised her hand. "I'll go tell him." Then, turning to her brother, she added, "Maybe he'll give us a ride in his car."

"Not until you finish your lunch." Shirley grabbed the child's hand and led her and Nicky back to the dining room.

Ruth stood watching the carriage house as the rest of the family went about their business. A dark figure passed the window inside. The shed wasn't heated, and that concrete floor must be ice cold.

Going back inside, she retrieved her coat and put it on, then grabbed Tucker's leather jacket from the hook. When she pushed the shed door open a moment later, she found Tucker bending over the engine, apparently checking the fluids.

"I thought you might need this," she said, holding his jacket out to him.

He put it on and thanked her, all the while managing to avoid eye contact with her. Without another word, he went back to what he'd been doing before she came in.

But Ruth wasn't so easily dismissed today. He wasn't going to brush her aside as he'd done last night.

"Aunt Ada thinks you love the stocking she made for you. It would break her heart if she knew otherwise."

His back still to her, Tucker rose and shut the hood. His knuckles whitened as he squeezed a fist and released it. "The stocking was fine."

Ruth walked around to where he stood and rested her hip against the fender of Aunt Shirley's El Dorado.

"Then what else is it? Was it something Aunt Ada did or said?"

Tucker pulled a handkerchief out of his back pocket and leaned over to wipe imaginary dirt from the hood. He was still avoiding her gaze. When he shook his head in response to her question, his dark hair fell forward, obscuring his face.

"In my experience, it doesn't pay to get too close to people." He moved the handkerchief idly over the fender. "I never intended to get involved with your family, much less become a part of it."

If Ruth had been confused before, she was bewildered now. "What does that have to do with a Christmas stocking?"

He stood up straight now. Shoving his hands into his coat pocket, he fixed his gaze on her. Ruth could see in his deep brown eyes that he was fighting a battle within himself.

"I don't believe I've ever told you what I do for a living."

Ruth felt her eyebrows draw together. What did this have to do with Aunt Ada's Christmas stocking?

"I'm a troubleshooter for Coastline Petroleum. Most of the time, my duties are fairly straightforward. Often, the solution to a problem involves pushing papers from one side of my desk to the other." He watched her intently, as if to make sure she was following what he said. "But sometimes, when the problems are too big, I have to eliminate jobs or let go of staff. And if those employees are my friends...well, the ties of friendship can bind my hands when that kind of change needs to be made."

Ruth waited for him to continue, wondering where this bit of his background was leading.

"When I came here, I didn't intend to celebrate Christmas, and I certainly didn't intend to get so involved in your family's activities. All I wanted was to spend some time alone."

"It's the way they are, Tucker. But if you felt as if they were infringing on your privacy, all you had to do was say so."

"It's not just that," he insisted. She could tell he was groping for the right words. "You people play for keeps. Your family's ties are extremely tight. There's commitment and permanence and standing invitations for Thanksgiving dinner and the Christmas reunion every year." He pushed the hair out of his face. "When your Aunt Ada gave me the stocking, it was like I was being formally adopted into the family."

"You're not the first," Ruth admitted, "and you probably won't be the last. There's a lot of love in this family...more than enough to go around." Her words, however, didn't seem to appease him.

"They're a wonderful group of people, but I'm not cut out to be a part of it."

The words were gentle, but their finality echoed through the small carriage house. Ruth shivered, and she knew it wasn't just the cold that caused the brittle ache inside her. When she spoke, her voice sounded strangely hollow. She only hoped he didn't hear the pain of rejection that tinged her words. Her family was so much a part of her that when he rejected them, he also rejected her. And the knowledge that it should matter so much surprised and frightened her. "So you're saying my family's ties are choking you."

Tucker turned to face her, the handkerchief dangling from his hand. "What I'm saying is that I've interfered with the Babcock family's reunion long enough. It's time I went home."

Ruth straightened and moved away from the El Dorado. "I don't recall anyone twisting your arm to stay." She hoped she didn't sound as bitter as she felt, and then she paused to wonder why the bitterness was there in the first place. Uncrossing her arms, she turned to the carriage house door.

Tucker stilled her with a hand on her elbow. That tiny gesture was enough to make her wish there was something she could say or do to keep him from leaving.

"It's not that I don't care for your family," he said. "I do. It's just that a situation has come up at work—"

"It's okay. You don't owe me any excuses. In fact, you don't owe any of us anything."

His hand slipped from her arm, and his expression hardened.

Ruth turned away, determined to let him walk out of their lives. She wasn't going to argue with him or, worse, let him see the void he was leaving in her family.

In *her*.

"You're right, I don't owe you any excuses. But I do owe you the truth."

She faced him once again and tried not to notice the way his brown eyes peered into her soul, stripping away all her defenses until her innermost thoughts seemed laid bare to his gaze. Ruth pulled her coat tighter around her midriff and crossed her arms in front of her, but the gesture did nothing to help her hide from his scrutiny.

"The truth is," he continued, "I'm not ready for a commitment."

Ruth felt her mouth drop open. He *had* seen inside her soul! "But I never—"

"I'm not ready to be 'Cousin' Tucker or accept the responsibilities and expectations that go with being a card-carrying family member."

He touched her arm again. "I hope you understand."

Ruth nodded. She didn't understand, but she wasn't so sure she wanted to. She gestured toward his convertible. "Don't you have a car better suited to winter? It seems like it would be cold riding around in that thing in this weather."

"It *is* cold, but that's the beauty of it."

She didn't think she'd ever understand men in general or Tucker in particular. Why would anyone choose aloneness over togetherness or traveling in the cold over traveling in warmth? Then again, weren't aloneness and coldness the same?

Ruth heard Tucker moving around in the room across the hall as she stripped the linens from the children's beds. She wondered if he would say good-bye before he left. Or would he disappear just as suddenly as he had appeared?

Almost as if her thoughts had caused him to materialize, she heard footsteps in the hall. The door pushed open, and a large form filled the door frame. Tucker had slung a duffel bag strap over one shoulder and tucked his jacket under the other arm. He looked the same as when he'd shown up a few nights ago, asking for a room at the inn. "I thought the kids might be in here. I wanted to tell them goodbye."

"They're packing up their things to go home later today."

It would be hard for the kids to go back to their home, wondering if they'd have to leave it soon. Leave a source of security in their young lives.

Ruth expected that Tucker's situation was quite different, but she couldn't help wondering if it wouldn't be hard for him to go back home, too. Would he miss the wisecracks and loving banter that filled this house?

Would he miss her?

As much as she was sure to miss him?

But she didn't ask the questions that were on her mind. Nor did she bother to wish him a merry Christmas, not after he'd been acting like such a humbug about the holiday. Instead, she said the first neutral thing that came to mind. "Have a safe trip."

"Thanks."

He took a half step forward, as if he might give her a very personal farewell. Was he going to kiss her? No, he stopped himself like a man noticing he was about to step on a copperhead snake.

As much as she hated the sense of regret that filled her, she realized he'd done the right thing. A goodbye kiss would only make things more difficult. "Would you like me to fix you a sandwich to take with you?"

It was the least she could do. But he merely shook his head. He held out his hand to her. "Walk downstairs with me while I find the kids and tell your family goodbye."

Chapter Seven

The rest of the family seemed genuinely sorry to see him go. Tucker supposed that Ruth was relieved. She'd wanted him out of here from the start. He probably should have taken the hint and left with his heart still locked safely away, but it was a little late for that now. At this point, he was mostly interested in damage control.

The plan was to start his good-byes with the children, then zip through the rest of the family and be gone before Aunt Shirley's lipstick was dry on his cheek, but the telephone interrupted him with a call from the Johnsons. While Ruth asked how Charles's interview had gone, Tucker gave each of the kids a hug and explained that he had to cut his visit short so he could take care of some business back home.

Then she called the children to the phone, where they shared the receiver, listening intently to what their parents had to say.

Ruth pulled Tucker aside and lowered her voice. "The Johnsons' car broke down. They're not going to be able to return today as planned."

Her brown eyes darkened, and Tucker could tell she was feeling the children's disappointment as if it were her own. He wanted to take her into his arms and kiss away the tiny worry line between her eyebrows. And he would have, except that such a response was exactly the reason he needed to leave. He cared too much about this family and the kids. And especially about Ruth. If he stayed, he would continue putting his heart at risk. Worse, Ruth might even come to feel the strings that pulled him to her. It was bad enough that his own sentiments had been compromised. It would be all the more tragic if she, too, became emotionally involved.

After he returned home to Alexandria, he could still wrap up the paperwork for the transaction he'd started here. The important thing right now was to get as much distance between him and the occupants of Willow Glen Plantation as possible. As soon as possible.

When the kids hung up, their little faces told exactly how they felt about this unexpected development. Nicky wore a scowl and took out his frustration by swatting at his sister's red-and-silver hair bow. The little one refused to rise to the bait, choosing instead to pop her thumb into her mouth.

Tucker knelt and hugged her. At the same time, he gave Nicky a reassuring pat on the shoulder.

Angie spoke around the thumb in her mouth. "Are you thtill going to leave uth?"

Tucker's heart constricted. Since he couldn't bring himself to answer her directly, he skirted the issue by focusing on their parents' return. "I'm sure your mom and dad can't wait to see you again. They'll be back as soon as they possibly can."

"Um, Tucker?" Ruth knelt beside him. "The Johnsons are stranded in Kentucky. The repair shop won't be able to get a replacement part until the day after Christmas." She gave the children a sympathetic smile. "And then it'll be another day to fix the car and drive home."

"*After* Christmas?"

She nodded.

This was exactly why he shouldn't have stayed as long as he had. When he came here, he hadn't planned to get caught up in a family's celebrations or tribulations. He'd only been seeking to escape from the harsh realities of the Christmas season.

But his sense of honor told him that his was a selfish reaction. So what if Aunt Ada had made him a bona fide, card-carrying member of the family by putting his stocking on the mantel with theirs? And so what if Ruth had somehow managed to unlock the part of his heart that he'd been trying so hard to protect?

It would hurt to stay and become further entrenched in the family, he was certain, especially the part where Ruth was involved. But it would hurt a whole lot less than what the kids were going through right now. Right now they were feeling abandoned and vulnerable. He couldn't bring himself to abandon them again.

It seemed as though Ruth was waiting with as much interest as the children for his answer to Angie's question.

Darting a tentative smile at the woman who had

come to mean so much to him in such a short time, he turned back to Angie and sacrificed his own Christmas for hers and Nicky's. "I suppose business can wait until your parents return."

He and Ruth rose to their feet together. She gave him a smile so warm and grateful that it alone outweighed whatever risks he took in prolonging his stay.

"Great," she said. "Then we'll have plenty of time for baking Christmas cookies."

The children's eyes lit up almost as bright as the Christmas tree in the parlor. But when Nicky caught Tucker's eye, his attitude suddenly changed. The boy lowered his voice to a manly octave and said to his sister, "Girls bake cookies. I'm going to help Tucker with that rug he promised to fix."

He looked to Tucker for affirmation. The two sets of female eyes followed the boy's gaze. Tucker had forgotten all about that curled corner of the rug. Although he'd done a temporary fix by duct-taping it to the floor, he needed to do it right with a strong carpet tape on the underside. Now, not only would he have to fulfill his promise to Aunt Shirley about fixing the rug, he'd also have to correct an attitude of the pint-size chauvinist. And the best way to do that was by example.

"A promise is a promise," he acknowledged to the dark-haired child. "But I hope Aunt Shirley doesn't mind if it waits until after I help with the cookies."

The boy's superior smile faded. "You're gonna bake cookies? With *girls?*"

"Sure. You don't get to lick the bowl until you've helped with the baking." At that, Tucker indulged in a daydream about licking batter off Ruth's fingers.

And maybe smearing some on her breasts and down to her flat stomach. Mmm, a feast fit for a king. A very *lucky* king.

Later that day, amid the cookie baking, rug repairing and horseplay in the yard with the kids, a large package arrived for Tucker. Despite the children's pleas to show them what was hidden inside the brown wrapper, he refused to reveal its contents. Instead, he took it out to the carriage house to lock it in his car.

Although his secretiveness was normal behavior at Christmas time, Ruth wondered if there was more going on than met the eye. After all, there'd been that strange phone call to his business associate asking to have something—probably that very package— shipped to him. And then he'd had that private discussion with Vivian, after which she'd rushed off to the bank. Was his secret package something that he had charmed his sister into buying? And if so, how much had he taken her for?

Although her head told her to keep her armor on around Tucker Maddock—for her own sake and for her family's—her heart once again told her to give him the benefit of the doubt. Whether it was due to the holiday goodwill or because she had become hopelessly and foolishly smitten with him, she wasn't certain, but Ruth did not press the matter. She only hoped she would not regret her decision later.

The children should be in their pajamas by now and waiting to be tucked into bed. On her way to their room, she almost collided with Tucker.

"Oops," he said, catching her by the arms. He didn't immediately let go, and Ruth had no desire for him to break the contact. "I was just going to say good night to the kids."

She hesitated, thinking about his role in diverting the children's attention away from their disappointment today. "It was very kind of you to stay…for the children's sake."

A heavy weight settled in her stomach as she acknowledged that he hadn't stayed for *her* sake.

"They're crazy about you," he said, allowing her to think for a moment that he might add his own sentiments to that statement. "And they'd have a good time here with you. But they miss their parents, and there was no way I'd add to their sense of loss. Especially not at Christmas."

Remembering what he'd said about losing his loved ones at Christmas, she wondered if that had played a role in his decision. And her heart once again went out to him.

She moved to the bedroom where Nicky and Angie were supposed to be settling into the twin beds. Tucker stopped her before she could push open the door.

"Tomorrow we need to go shopping again with the children."

"On Christmas Eve? It'll be a madhouse."

One corner of Tucker's mouth pulled into a tight line as he seemed to weigh his words. "Nicky was pleased with the craft projects you showed him how to make for the rest of the family, but he needs to get one more gift…a special one."

For her, Ruth knew without asking. And she was touched by the thoughtfulness, both Nicky's and Tucker's.

"And you and I need to get some gifts for him and Angie to open on Christmas morning."

"Yes, that's a good idea." She had already planned to make a hasty trip before the crowds hit the mall. This way she and Tucker could find out the children's preferences, then separate while one bought the gifts and the other kept the children too occupied to notice.

She had worked so hard to make this a perfect Christmas for her family. She would do no less for Nicky and Angie.

Tucker accompanied her into the room to get the children settled into bed, but they were still wired up by all the Christmas activities that day. And Angie was worried that Santa Claus wouldn't be able to find them away from their own home.

Ruth sat on the little girl's bed and tried to reassure her. "Don't you worry. There will be something for you here on Christmas morning, and then you can have Christmas again with your parents after you go home."

"But how will he find us?"

"Well, there's a special thing at this time of year...something called Christmas magic."

Angie poked her thumb in her mouth while Nicky and Tucker watched in amusement. "I don't bewieve in magic."

Ruth sighed. By the time children came to her fourth-grade class, they'd already arrived at their own conclusions as to how the presents arrived in their living rooms on Christmas morning. She was stumped as to what to tell the child.

"Smart girl," Tucker said, effectively undermining Ruth's efforts to comfort her. He sat on the bed behind

Ruth, his knee grazing the back of her thigh. "You want a scientific answer?"

Angie nodded, and he launched into a lengthy explanation of global positioning devices and how they work. Ruth thought for sure he'd give himself away when he mentioned the Pythagorean theorem, microwaves and the ozone layer all in the same breath, but Angie hung on every word.

In fact, he almost had *her* believing his cockamamie tale. It was easy to see how Aunt Shirley, Vivian and the others had fallen so readily under his spell. The man sure had a knack for reeling them in.

"How about a bedtime story?" Ruth asked, and pulled out her favorite classroom fiction.

"I've already heard that one," Nicky said.

Tucker didn't help matters by pointing out that a book about wizards wasn't exactly in keeping with the Christmas spirit. He left the room and came back a few minutes later with two books in his hand and a triumphant smile on his face. "These were still in the attic, right where the Newlands used to keep all their Christmas stuff."

Lifting Angie, he carried her to Nicky's bed and sat in the middle with a child on each side of him. He patted the mattress beside his legs, indicating that Ruth should join him.

She did, and was overcome with the feeling of family togetherness that emanated from the situation. A more intimate vision came to her in which she and Tucker were snuggled together in a big, comfy bed with their children nestled around them.

Immediately aware of the folly in letting her

thoughts continue to follow that course, she snapped her attention back to what Tucker was saying.

"Every year, Mr. and Mrs. Newland read *The Night Before Christmas* to Chris and me the night before Christmas Eve," he told the children as he showed them the Clement Moore story of St. Nicholas. "And then on Christmas Eve, just to make sure we remembered what the holiday was all about, they read us this one." This time, he held up a children's picture book about the birth in Bethlehem. "So we'll continue the tradition."

His voice reverberated, deep and masculine, as he described the eight tiny reindeer and the old elf's "bowl full of jelly."

The pleasant sound wound its way into her psyche, and Ruth felt her defenses slip away. As she sat there on the bed, her heart laid bare to Tucker's occasional glances that served to shepherd her into the cozy group, she tried to imagine him as a young boy.

Ruth had taken to Nicky, probably much the way Mrs. Newland had welcomed Tucker into her life. But Nicky's hardships were more financial than familial. Ruth suspected, by Tucker's lack of discussion of the subject, that his genetic family ties were minimal, at best. Why else would parents have let their child spend such an important holiday with someone else every year? Why would they allow another family to share special moments like this? Moments that bonded their son with another family in tradition and memories?

She now knew without a doubt that Tucker had been telling the truth about coming here to recapture those memories. It was clear that he also had something else—another agenda, perhaps—going on as well, but that was not the reason he had returned to Willow Glen Plantation.

He was a man who was aching with a need deep in his heart. And, with blinding clarity, Ruth knew exactly how she was going to help him fill that need.

Christmas Day had greeted them with warmer temperatures, and it was a good thing since the children had needed to take their new puppy outside a half dozen times already.

Ruth accompanied them on their latest trip to the backyard. And, although Tucker had been unaccountably quiet for much of the afternoon, he joined them as well.

She slipped a hand under her open jacket and once again touched the gold pin on her thin sweater. Tucker had given each of the ladies in the family a pin suited to their individual personalities or hobbies. The uniqueness of each revealed the amount of thought and the time spent searching for the gift that was a perfect fit.

Ruth's pin, a gold "A+," reflected her role as a teacher. Or did it have other connotations as well? She turned to the man beside her and studied him. His attention was fixed on the children, his Adam's apple bobbing slightly as he laughed silently at their antics. As far as she was concerned, he deserved an A + + for his role in helping make this a happy Christmas for them.

And for her.

Dropping her hands to her sides, she was reminded of the flat box in her pants pocket...the gift she had yet to give to Tucker.

He turned toward her, and their gazes met. Since last night, Ruth had begun to see him in a fresh light. With her new perspective, she brazenly studied his face. The deep brown eyes that seemed to be far too aware of her as a woman, the slight curve of his nose that hinted at a rough football tackle, and lips that reminded her how tender and sweet he'd been each time he kissed her.

She dropped her gaze in a feeble attempt to steer her thoughts away from such dangerous territory. His battery-powered necktie blinked its red and white bulbs from the painted-on Christmas tree.

She smiled. "The kids are thrilled that you decided to wear their tie first."

He matched her smile. "With at least six new ones to choose from, it was a hard decision."

Almost everyone, including Ruth, had arrived at the same idea, but for varying reasons. The older family members had given ties because tradition practically dictated it. Ruth's choice had more to do with keeping things neutral between them by avoiding an overly personal gift. Until, of course, she came across the one that now resided in her pocket. Vivian, on the other hand, had seemed intent on making her tie as personal as possible by reaching around his neck from behind to help him knot it. Then again, Ruth might have been overreacting to their closeness.

Only Aunt Ada and Uncle Oren had broken the pattern. Ada had hooked a small rug to place beside his bed, and Oren had given him a fire extinguisher to keep in his sports car.

She turned and watched the children roll on the ground with the puppy. Angie giggled delightedly as

"Tucky" gave her face an enthusiastic tongue washing. The moniker was a blend of Tucker's name and the state where their parents were waiting for their car to be fixed.

"You've made quite a few people very happy by arranging to give them that dog," Ruth said, ticking them off on her fingers. "The kids, obviously. The Foutches because that's one fewer of Bitsy's pups they'll have to find a home for. I just hope the Johnsons will be able to find a place to live that's suitable for keeping a dog."

"When I called them to suggest the idea, Charles said they would find a way to make it work." He broke off to warn Nicky not to let the dog tug on his sock. "And if the job in Kentucky falls through, I'll see what I can do about finding him some work at my company."

"Well, you've certainly helped make the children's Christmas special, even if their parents weren't here to celebrate it with them."

He stared across the yard, his brown eyes darkening as if a cloud had passed overhead. "Christmas memories should be happy ones," he stated flatly.

Silence hung heavily for a few seconds as Ruth waited for him to continue. She didn't want to pry, but when he remained silent, curiosity and probably a tad too much concern—got the best of her. "What about your family, Tucker? You've spoken of the Newlands, but—"

"The Newlands were my family," he said with an edge of sharpness. When she flinched at his tone, he seemed to reconsider his response. "My happiest years were with them.'' He closed his eyes momentarily, as if resisting an unwanted trip into his past.

When he opened them again, his expression had softened somewhat. ''When I was small, my mother was very sick. She tried not to let me know. Tried to make me laugh even when she was so weak she couldn't stand.''

Unable to help herself, Ruth moved nearer to him. A man like Tucker did not handle sympathy well, but she touched his arm, hoping that she could help absorb some of his pain by the light contact. To her relief, he did not pull away.

''She died when I was Angie's age...a few days before Christmas.'' He clenched his fingers, then appearing to notice the telltale action, relaxed them. ''My father coped by drinking his paychecks away, which meant I had to go to school in rags worse than what Nicky and Angie brought with them. Dad always got worse around the anniversary of her death, and eventually he didn't even bother putting up a tree or buying presents.''

His voice softened ever so slightly. ''My father died of cirrhosis of the liver on Christmas Day in my senior year of high school. I guess his timing wasn't altogether bad. His insurance money enabled me to go to college.''

''Oh, Tucker, I had no idea.''

''You don't need to feel sorry for me. If things hadn't got that bad at home, I might never have known the kind of family experience I had with Chris's family.''

The knot of sympathy that had grown in her chest upon hearing about his childhood clutched a little tighter as he sought the positive in his unfortunate past.

Ruth took a breath. "My parents died when Vivian and I were very young. I barely remember them. We were fortunate Aunt Shirley was willing to take us both in to raise. She was widowed at the time, and I think she waited this long before dating again because of us."

Tucker cleared his throat. "She's a good woman. And she's still making sure you're taken care of." He paused. "In ways that you can't even begin to imagine."

She nodded her agreement. "Whenever I felt bad about not having a father figure in my life, I remembered all her sacrifices. But as much as I appreciate all she's done for me, I still want my future children to grow up with two parents."

He gave her a gentle smile and lifted a hand to her elbow. "I wish that for you, too, Ruth."

The way he said it almost made her wonder if he had someone specific in mind. She wondered if now would be an appropriate time to give him his other gift.

"Come here," he said. "I want to show you something." He urged her toward the carriage-house garage. When she hesitated, he explained, "The kids'll be all right for a couple of minutes, and we can keep an eye on them through the window."

As they stepped inside, she supposed he might want to show her the new fire extinguisher he'd received. But that was odd, because she'd already seen the gift this morning.

He popped the trunk and withdrew a large brown

box…the same one that had been delivered two days ago.

"I know you were planning for this to be your family's most perfect Christmas ever, and, well, I sort of messed that up by crashing into the middle of it."

Ashamed of her uncharitable reaction to his arrival, Ruth started to protest, but he silenced her by placing the package on the hood of his car and motioning for her to open it.

"It's not much," he told her, "but I hope it helps make up for some of the inconvenience I may have caused you."

Now she really felt bad. It had never been her intent to make him feel unwelcome…only to protect her family. Yet she had hurt his feelings. What a very un-Christmaslike attitude.

"Go ahead, open it. I think you'll like it." He smiled, his expression so open and warm that Ruth wondered why she had ever doubted him in the first place.

Taking care not to scratch the paint on his car, she ripped the paper away and eased open the box lid. Inside, arranged in neat rows and stacks, were assorted train cars and tracks. A zippered bag held miniature trees, people and railroad crossing signs, and tucked away in the corner of the box were the buildings for a tiny town.

Ruth crossed her hands over her chest. Her vision blurred as she stepped back to admire the exquisitely detailed pieces, and she fought to blink away the mist in her eyes.

"You're in luck," he said when she couldn't find the words to tell him how much she liked his thoughtful gift. "It's now considered politically correct for girls to play with trains."

The mist pooled in her eyes and spilled onto her cheeks. She met his gaze, not bothering to brush away the evidence of her emotional response. When she was finally able to speak, her voice was barely audible, even to herself. "How did you know?"

"Let's just say Santa Claus told me." Taking her hands in his, he rubbed his fingers over her knuckles. "I hope you like it."

"It's wonderful," she assured him, thinking the one-word description applied to the giver as well. "The pieces are so intricate…they look like they must be antique."

"Mr. Newland's father gave the set to him one Christmas, then he passed it on to Chris many years later." A speck of sadness briefly clouded Tucker's smile. "Last year it became mine. And now it's yours."

She gasped as the enormity of his gift sank in. "Oh, Tucker, you shouldn't have—"

"I want you to have it." When she tried to resist, he told her, "It belongs with you…and your daughter, and your daughter's daughter."

"Tucker, I don't know what to say." On impulse, she stretched up to give him a kiss on the cheek. Well, she'd told herself she was aiming for his cheek, but somewhere between thinking it and doing it, her lips went off course and landed on his mouth. And once they made contact, it was as if neither could break away.

Still standing on tiptoe, Ruth felt herself being pulled into the circle of his arms. His big hands cradling her back, she allowed herself to melt against his body, her chest pressed intimately against his as they tasted the nectar of each other's kiss.

Easily dwarfed by his size and power, Ruth felt neither intimidated nor overwhelmed. Rather, it was the sensation of sinking into the warm embrace of a large featherbed. The gentle caress of his lips against hers and the tender pressure of his fingers against her spine entranced her, luring her to a place that was so wonderful it must surely be dreamland.

When he deepened the kiss, she welcomed the blurry delight of losing herself in the precious headiness of it. If a kiss like this could be bottled and sold, demand for it would far exceed that of alcohol and other mind-altering drugs. But it was so much more addictive.

Having sampled the thrill of his kiss, Ruth craved more. Since that first time under the holly, she had progressed to wanting a daily fix. And now she found herself desiring a much more potent form of his loving attention. But she knew in her heart that once she succumbed to such a pleasure, she would be hooked for life.

With immense regret, Ruth became aware that Tucker was ending their prolonged kiss. He must have had a similar feeling, she decided, as he breathed a wistful sigh against her mouth.

The dusty rose shade of lipstick was smeared across his mouth and on the gray shading of his five o'clock shadow. Unlike the primly puckered peach prints that Aunt Shirley left in her wake, these sensual slide marks gave evidence of Ruth's raw yearnings.

Reaching up, she wiped away the telltale sign of their mutual attraction.

"Thank you," she said after her breathing became more even. It wasn't clear, even to herself, whether she was referring to the train set or his kiss. Probably both.

"Thank *you*." He obviously took it to mean the latter.

"I have something for you." His appreciative gaze followed her gesture as she reached into her pants pocket, prompting her to clarify her statement. "A Christmas present."

Withdrawing the thin box, she fluffed the gold ribbon that had been flattened while in her pocket and handed the package to him.

"But you already gave me a gift," he protested.

"This is much better than any old tie. Go ahead and open it."

He did as she asked and withdrew a yellowed envelope, stained with blood. Respecting his privacy, she had left the envelope sealed. Ruth watched as his gaze swept over the parchment. The paper was covered with mock legalese and carried two scrawled signatures at the bottom, one of them Tucker Maddock's.

Holding it at arm's length, he stared dazedly at the memento from his past. He sniffed and self-consciously cleared his throat, then carefully tore open the seal. With an officious tone and fond smile, he read aloud the terms of the blood-brothers' pact. They had promised themselves as brothers for life...a life that had been much too short for one of them.

When he looked up from the paper, the memory still

reflected in his expression, Ruth knew her desire to help fulfill his Christmas wish had been achieved.

Wordlessly, he opened his arms, and she stepped into them. She laid her head against his firm chest and was aware of his cheek resting against her hair.

"I started out thinking this would be just another horrible Christmas," he confessed. "But because of you, it's turning out to be perfect."

Chapter Eight

The children were now pining for their parents, and Tucker was pining for something that he couldn't quite name. Or maybe it was something that he just refused to acknowledge. Whatever the case, it was a much simpler matter to distract Nicky and Angie from their hearts' longing than to quiet the voice that clamored within his own soul. If luck was with him, playing in the newly fallen snow might still the restlessness in his heart.

A snowball exploded on the back of his neck. The park was filled with the town's children trying out their new toboggans and sleds, but Tucker knew exactly who had lobbed the powdery missile. Scooping up a handful of the stuff, he wadded it into a loose ball and pegged his ten-year-old rival square in the chest.

"Hey, I didn't do it," Nicky protested, but Tucker pelted him again. "Miss Ruth started it."

Tucker halted his counterassault and turned in the direction Nicky pointed. Ruth, looking sweet and demure in her pale gray coat and pink stocking cap, grinned innocently, and waggled her gloved fingers at him. And then whacked him on the shoulder with a snowball she had hidden behind her back.

Surprise quickly gave way to revenge. As Tucker stooped to replenish his ammunition and return the volley, another snowball hit him on the seat of the pants, compliments of Nicky. A melee broke out, with snowballs flying in all directions, puffs of loose snow ineffectually flung by little Angie, and Tucky the beagle barking and chasing the snowballs as if they were tennis balls flung for his benefit.

Laughing and breathing hard, they continued for another ten minutes with Angie perched on Tucker's shoulders for a better vantage point from which to bean Nicky, Ruth or Brooke. He and Ruth soon ran out of steam, but Nicky was just getting started. Abandoning them for more lively action with some of his friends from school, the boy went off to join in their game of "stealth snowball." Angie, on the other hand, was ready for quiet play, so he, Ruth and Brooke helped her get started building a snowman. And when the little girl struck up a camaraderie with another child, the two adults retreated to a small patch of unspoiled snow where they could watch and catch their breath.

Standing quietly, Tucker took a moment to enjoy the view. Not the sloping ground where all ages and sizes of people scooted downhill on everything from designer sleds to trashcan lids and cardboard boxes, and not the view of the ice-crusted lake that glistened in the distance. Rather, he enjoyed the side view of the young woman beside him whose cheeks and nose shone a bright pink from the cold and exertion. Her chest rose and fell in a steady rhythm as she gazed at the young people engaged in their play.

"That was fun," he said at last. "Thanks for instigating it."

"Moi?" she asked in false innocence, and splayed a hand across her chest. "Whatever makes you think I would do such a thing?"

Tucker's response was a raised eyebrow and a quirk of his mouth.

"I'm glad Brooke came with us," she declared. "The poor thing was going stir-crazy in the house with all those relatives."

He grinned as he remembered the teen's often-spoken lament that it would be another "eighteen whole months" before she'd finally have her driver's license and thus her freedom.

"Yeah, it's too bad Vivian didn't come, too. She would have had a great time if she'd just given it a try." What he didn't say, however, was that he suspected she didn't want to break a nail or mess up her carefully styled hairdo. The contrast between the two women made him appreciate Ruth's zest and enthusiasm all the more.

Ruth's eyes frosted over at mention of her sister's name.

"What?" he said.

She paused for a significant moment. "Nothing, I'm just tired."

Tired of what, he wasn't sure, but he had a strong feeling she was not referring to the after-effects of their snowball fight. If there was something going on between the siblings, he didn't want to get in the middle of it. So he opted to take her comment at face value. "Want to sit down?" He pointed toward a flattened box someone had left behind. "We could sit on that cardboard and stay dry."

She glanced toward the box, then fixed her attention on the pristine patch of snow behind them. "Have you ever made a snow angel?"

He followed her gaze and avoided answering what was on his mind. He didn't need to make a snow angel because one already existed. With flecks of snow clinging to her jacket and stocking cap, this dark-haired angel needed only a pair of wings to complete the picture.

As with any heavenly entity, she had high expectations. She had worked hard to ensure that her family enjoyed a perfect Christmas this year...or as close to perfect as possible. She'd been quite vocal about that particular desire. But he knew, without her saying so, that she had a long-term goal she was intent on achieving. Ever the traditionalist, she wouldn't be happy with less than a committed, family-minded husband and a slew of kids to call their own. The problem, he knew, would be to find a man who was worthy of her love. Tucker doubted that such a creature existed. Still, he hoped that someday her dreams would be realized. Of course, if there weren't so much at risk—namely, his heart—he might have even considered pursuing the possibility himself.

"No, I haven't," he said, shaking the previous thought from his head.

"Well, there's a first time for everything."

Tucker gulped in response, then realized she was referring to the snow angel.

"Come here, I'll show you how," she said, grasping his hand and standing at arm's length from him. "First, you have to work up your nerve."

That was an understatement.

"And then you just fall into it. Simple as that." She demonstrated by making a two-part landing, first on her rear, and then on her back. A little "oof" escaped as her shoulders hit the snow, proving that the process wasn't totally without its hazards.

He followed her lead, then lay beside her with their fingers touching. He wished their gloves weren't there so he could touch her hand directly. In fact, he wanted to touch more than just her hand. He wanted to touch all of her...except her heart, of course. Because, as they'd proved a moment ago, that would hurt too much when they fell. Simple as that. Only, it wasn't so simple.

"And then you spread your wings," she said, slowly moving her arms up and down to form the fanned image of wings in the snow beside her, "and soar to the heights of ecstasy."

And, when the soaring was done, he mentally finished for her, they'd plummet back to reality and land with a heart-jarring thump. At least, that had always been his experience...especially around Christmas.

"There, isn't that beautiful?" she said, looking at the winged formations they'd created.

Tucker studied the swirled snow beside him and then fixed his gaze on the woman who'd turned his life upside down in only a week. "Yes, it's beautiful," he admitted, "but it'll only last a short time before it all melts away into nothingness."

She laughed, her soft voice tinkling like a Christmas bell. "Do you always see the glass as half empty?"

Tucker sighed. "My glass has been broken enough times that I don't count on it anymore to quench my thirst."

Ruth fell silent for a moment. "I know it might sound kind of hokey, especially considering what we're doing right now," she told him, "but I think we have to trust our angels to protect us from what we fear."

He turned to face her and felt a clump of snow work its way down his collar. "You mean, like when losing a mother? Or being abandoned by an alcoholic father?"

There was no anger in his voice...only a begrudging resolve to accept his fate and not expect any special treatment on his behalf.

"Or when three of the kindest and most loving people who ever lived were taken away all at once? No thanks. I'll take my fate in my own hands." And protect himself by avoiding whatever dangers lurked in his path.

And dear, sweet Ruth ranked high on his list of hazards.

"Oh, Tucker," she breathed softly. "You're not protecting yourself from your fears. You're protecting yourself from living."

Did he say "just a minute" or "come on in?" Ruth could have sworn it was the latter. Balancing the train track segments in her hands, she pushed Tucker's bedroom door open with her hip.

Inside, Tucker froze in the midst of pulling off his undershirt. He stood barefoot in the middle of the room, wearing only a pair of Black Watch plaid boxers and holding the shirt in front of him as if deciding whether to continue undressing or put it back on.

"I'm sorry, I thought you said to come in."

"No, that's okay," he said, tossing the shirt on the far side of the bed, where it fell to the floor, and grabbing for a pair of drawstring pajama bottoms. He pulled them on quickly, but his actions were not those of someone who'd been caught...well, with his pants down. In fact, he didn't seem at all embarrassed as he tied the strings at his waist.

Ruth watched, transfixed, as he crossed the room to the small chest of drawers and pulled out a clean undershirt. His skin had a healthy glow despite the loss of his summer tan, leading her to wonder if he had some Mediterranean blood. His shoulders seemed even wider without shirtsleeves to hide their breadth, and the light smattering of soft brown hair failed to conceal the pectoral definition of his chest. His torso angled enticingly from his deep rib cage to his narrow waist. With a quick flick and a tug, Tucker covered himself with a sleeveless undershirt that made his shoulders look fuller and his abdomen even flatter. Just in time, too, considering the direction in which Ruth's gaze had been going.

"You wanted something?" he asked.

Oh, yes, indeed! "I was wondering if you could give me a little demonstration." Above and beyond the one he'd already given her, that is. She lifted the track parts for him to see. "Could you show me how to hook these so they don't come apart when the train rolls over them?"

He took one of the track segments, his hand brushing hers as he did so, and walked over to the bed, where he sat down and started fidgeting with the connecting part. Ruth joined him there and held her bit of track while he joined their ends.

"In addition to making sure the prongs are lined up," he explained as he pointed to a movable part she hadn't noticed before, "you have to latch this small piece onto the adjoining one."

Ruth leaned closer to get a better look. He smelled of cologne and soap. She stared past the track in his hand to the intriguing hollows where chest muscle met ribs. He'd mentioned before that he worked in an office, but she doubted he got his bulk from pushing papers around. He didn't seem the type to mindlessly lift weights. Probably boxed instead.

Her fingers itched to test the hardness of his arms. His thick biceps bunched with each movement of his hand. He was talking as he showed her how to fit the pieces together, but she didn't hear the words...only the soft rumble of his voice and the squeak of the bedframe beneath their weight.

She leaned closer still, her eyes refusing to focus on the toy as the darkly masculine scent of him dulled her brain. Gosh, she wished... She didn't know what she wished. Only that she wanted something. And that *something* involved Tucker.

"I must be boring you. Your eyes are glazed over."

Ruth's gaze lifted to the dark brown of his irises. She licked her lips. She was aware that he gazed back at her, but she couldn't bring herself to respond verbally to his comment. She attempted to form the words, but her lips insisted on drawing themselves into a speechless pucker.

"I was thinking the same thing," he told her.

He lowered his head to hers at the same time she rose to meet him. Once again, it was the best thing she'd ever experienced. How could he keep doing that? How could he keep surpassing the kisses they'd already shared?

Her hands automatically went around that wonderfully slim waist, and after a moment Tucker lay on his back. Her weight was braced against his torso as she let her fingertips explore the firm taper of his waist. He seemed content to let her be the aggressor, mirroring for her whatever she did to him.

Ruth's roaming fingers grazed the cotton strings at his waistband. Without thinking about what she was doing, she tangled the fabric around her fingers and slowly pulled. Tucker responded by hooking two fingers inside her jeans and unfastening the snap with a flick of his thumb. Then the zipper parted with the downward pressure of his hand. He didn't release his hold, but pulled her closer, the backs of his fingers grazing an area that sought to be included in the giddying thrill of his attention.

A small gasp escaped her throat, and she gave a frantic yank at his drawstring. Tucker's kisses were wonderfully satisfying, but she wanted so much more.

His lips stilled, and she was vaguely aware that he'd stopped breathing. With a boldness she'd never known before, Ruth allowed her touch to follow the arrow of hair that trailed from his belly button to his waistband...and beyond.

There was no question that he wanted her as much as she desired him. She pressed closer, urging him with the movement of her body to take their mutual attraction to its logical—or not-so-logical—conclusion.

The clip in her hair had failed to contain the chestnut curls that now swept Tucker's face. Having swept aside the soft curtain of hair, he began trailing kisses down her throat to that sensitive spot at the hollow of her neck. A sound, low and long, rose from her throat. And when his hand closed over her breast, inciting a tumult within her body, she let him know without any words being spoken that she wanted him to take her...take all of her.

Tucker rolled her onto her back. Leaning on one elbow, he hovered over her, one leg draped across the lower half of her body. Those wonderful pectoral muscles grazed her chest, and Ruth cursed the clothes that prevented her from feeling them sliding, skin to skin, across the tender tips of her nipples. He grasped her hip and pulled her close so that his hardness pressed against her lower belly. Instinctively, Ruth arched closer, wishing she could speed up or slow down the passage of time at will.

"Are you sure you want to do this?"

Tucker's face was only inches from hers, and she lifted her face to press an answering kiss to his lips. "Yes." When he hesitated, as if unsure whether to take her at her word, she added, "Now."

He slid his hand under the hem of her shirt and idly stroked her bare belly while he seemed to ponder her answer. ''I'm not prepared to offer you a commitment. Whatever we share tonight is for the moment only,'' he said at last. ''I'm going to be gone in a few days.''

Though his reason was unspoken, she suspected he was refusing to give his heart away yet again, only to risk losing her love just as he'd lost all his other loved ones in his past.

It was too late to protect her own heart. It already belonged to him. She'd known that—but refused to admit it—even before the first time he'd ever kissed her.

Ruth had fallen in love with him. She could not protect herself from the pain of loss as Tucker was seeking to do, but she'd rather have the memory of one night with him than nothing at all.

''I'm not asking for any promises.'' She covered his hand with hers and pushed it upward, under her sweater to continue the maddening circles he'd been drawing on her skin. ''Just make love to me.''

He studied her face for an excruciatingly long moment, as if deciding whether to follow through with her suggestion. Her plea. But then his roaming hand found and released the front clasp of her bra, and his fingers closed around the soft flesh of her breast. At that point, it seemed as though the decision was made for him.

He helped Ruth remove her sweater and jeans. In response, Ruth pushed his skin-hugging white shirt up so that she could feel his strength. His warmth. His appeal.

''I apologize if I seem clumsy at this,'' she said. ''Perhaps you could guide me through it since this is my first time.''

Tucker drew his hand away from her as if he'd been doused with ice water. The thin sheen of perspiration on his forehead suddenly turned cold, and he felt goose bumps sprout on his body. Not the good kind of goose bumps. The scary kind. Her words were a cold-water reminder that Ruth was a woman who played for keeps.

She had assured him she wasn't asking for any promises. She had practically begged him to finish making love to her. Any other man would gladly accept her words without reading anything into them. But Tucker knew that if he followed through with his body's desires, they would become irrevocably bonded to each other. This wouldn't just be casual sex. It would be a forever kind of thing…for both of them.

Although his body urged him to reconsider, he knew it would be wrong to string Ruth along without any promises. He remembered their discussion at the park earlier today and thought how, once again, his guardian angels were letting him down. Why hadn't they stepped in sooner, before either of them could be hurt?

"What's the matter?" she asked. Her eyebrows were pulled together, and the confusion was evident in her beautiful face. "Did I do something wrong? If I did, just show me the right way to make love." Her voice was still husky with passion, and he got turned on all over again. "I'm willing to learn."

"No, it's not that. You're perfect just as you are." The last thing he wanted to do was make her feel bad about herself when it was he who should be feeling bad for having let things go this far.

"Then what?" There was no impatience in her

voice. Only concern for him. Concern that he didn't deserve.

"This is wrong." He sat up on the bed, pulled his shirt on and fastened the tie at his waist. Then he handed her the green sweater and jeans he'd helped her remove earlier. "We shouldn't be doing this. It's wrong of me to take advantage of you when I'm not willing to make any promises in return."

Although she had once again covered herself, temptation had not been removed for Tucker. Now he knew the treasures that lay beneath the ordinary-looking clothes that covered her body. He would never be able to look at her again without remembering the firm, smooth feel of her belly or the puckered pink tips of her breasts that tantalized him with their eager response to his touch.

Annoyed by his reaction, he got up and walked to the door. All he'd accomplished by allowing things to go this far was a lot of frustration...for both of them. Just as he'd feared, his involvement with this family—and especially with Ruth—was becoming more entangled. Their ties were becoming so knotted he might never be able to separate himself from them.

Frowning, she finished straightening her clothes and followed him to the door. Tucker could tell he'd hurt her much more than he'd anticipated.

"Does this have anything to do with Vivian?" she asked.

"Vivian?" Why on earth would she think he was interested in her sister? And then he remembered what she'd said about her boyfriends all dumping her for Vivian. "Good grief, no," he told her. "It has to do with you."

Chapter Nine

Ruth pushed the "jump" button, and her character leaped from the cliff, bringing a quick end to the game she'd been playing. A simulated cloud of smoke arose from the tangle of digital legs and arms, and the synthesized voice made a weary moan.

"This is too hard," she declared, realizing too late that she sounded like some of her students who wanted quick and easy solutions to their homework problems. She set the handheld electronic game aside. Heck, this wasn't school—unless she considered it the school of hard knocks—and her problem was more complicated than finding the common denominator in a math assignment. "What else do you have that's easier?"

Without looking up from the Lincoln log house that he was helping Angie build, Nicky pointed to the coffee table where a couple of game cartridges rested near a stack of papers and Vivian's purse.

Despite her efforts to the contrary, Ruth's thoughts

kept going back to last night. After Tucker had realized how condemning his words had sounded to her, he had tried to explain that he was only referring to her need for a permanent man in her life.

She'd never told him any such thing, so his excuse seemed weak at best. Perhaps, as with all the other guys who'd had their heads turned by Vivian, it *was* about Ruth. Perhaps it was about whatever she lacked that prevented them from staying interested in her.

She sighed and rose to her feet. Her foot and ankle had gone numb from when she'd been sitting on the floor. Ruth shook her foot like a cat exiting a sandbox. With any luck, maybe the numbness would spread to her heart.

Picking up both game cartridges from the table, she read the descriptions printed on the back of the cartons. One, like the first, required a lot of strategy to get to each succeeding level. Apparently, her strategy left a lot to be desired. The other involved guiding puzzle pieces down a chute until they fit together tightly. Ruth doubted she'd ever be proficient at putting the pieces together, but she'd rather worry over this particular puzzle than the real-life one that currently commanded so much of her emotional energy.

Laying the strategy game back on the table, Ruth paused at the official-looking paper beside Vivian's purse. Though it was folded, a portion of a signature peeked out at her. "R. Tucker M—."

Chancing a glance around the room, she saw that the children were still occupied with their miniature log cabin. Aunt Ada was already needlepointing an Easter basket using stiff plastic canvas.

Feigning nonchalance, Ruth eased to the sofa and

picked up the document. Turning it over, she noticed another signature. "Shirley Babcock Givens."

Oh, heavens! What had her aunt done now?

With a hurried shake of the paper, she flipped it fully open. At the top of the front sheet were the words Deed of Trust. Below that were the address and description of Willow Glen Plantation. Ruth felt sick to her stomach.

"I don't think you should be looking at that," Ada May said in gentle admonition. "It belongs to Vivian and Cousin Tucker."

Ruth shot Aunt Ada a look that would have sent one of her more timid students running for cover.

The older woman shrugged and resumed her needlework. "Well, they put it there after they got back from taking Shirley to town this morning. So I assume it's theirs."

That would explain the notary signature and seal. They'd probably been to the lawyer to make the transfer official.

Ruth sagged against the back of the sofa. It was bad enough that her gullible aunt had been duped. But Vivian should have known better. Had her head been so turned by Tucker's charm and good looks that she couldn't think clearly? Goodness knows, Ruth knew only too well how easy it was for such a thing to happen.

"It's all right if I read it," she told Aunt Ada, "because it concerns me."

In fact, it concerned all of them. Without a place for Shirley to live, the family would have to help find a solution for this dilemma. As for herself, she could rent an apartment or small house, possibly even closer to school. But it was *this* house that she loved…with its history, its warmly inviting atmosphere, and its convenience for family gatherings.

With the sale of the house, Vivian would have to find a new place to live, too. Ruth remembered finding her and Tucker on the side porch, and Vivian's hasty trip to the bank. It was now obvious that her sister had been helping to facilitate the sale. Why had she been a willing participant? Had Tucker proposed to her and promised to whisk her away on a white steed to his castle? And if he was romancing Vivian, why had he come so close to whisking Ruth away last night?

She became aware of someone entering the room and looked up from the paper she'd been reading. Tucker and Vivian stopped short when they saw what she held in her hand. Their faces told her everything she needed to know. It was clear they'd both been striving to keep this a secret from her. And now that their secret had been outed, they looked like startled deer in a rifle scope.

"Uh-oh," said Vivian. She turned and left the room.

"Oops, I'm all out of 'misty meadow' yarn," Aunt Ada announced. Picking up her bulging bag of needlework supplies, she hastened out as quickly as her orthopedic shoes would allow.

The children and dog, probably the only innocent ones in the room, seemed unaware of the tension that crackled around them. She had to give Tucker credit. At least he didn't turn tail and flee as the other two had.

He stood his ground, shoulders squared and a hint of a grin smeared across his face.

Ruth stood, prepared to let him have it for taking advantage of her family. "I think I already know what's going on," she told him with a rattle of the paper, "but I'd like to hear it directly from you."

If she thought he had hurt her last night, she quickly realized this was an even greater pain. Not only had he enticed and then rejected her, but now he had betrayed her as well. She swallowed hard to keep the tremor out of her voice.

"The truth, please."

"Nothing but," he replied, as if he wouldn't dream of deceiving her.

A car pulled up the drive and swung into the parking area.

Angie jumped up from her play and ran to the window, the puppy at her heels. "It's Mama and Daddy!"

Nicky dropped the fence he'd been working on and ran with his little sister to the front door. Ruth heard the door pull open just as the bell sounded.

Squeals of excitement filled the air as parents and children rejoiced in their family reunion. Still clutching the document, Ruth wagged it at Tucker. "You may have been saved by the bell, but I still expect answers later."

Then she stepped past him and joined the rest of the group in the foyer where hugs and kisses were being freely exchanged. It was probably just as well that the Johnsons had arrived when they did, she thought. The delay in the confrontation about the sale of Aunt Shirley's house would allow Ruth to clear her head first.

To her dismay, the source of her problems followed her to the front hall. Tucker greeted and invited the parents into the parlor as if he were a long-standing member of the family.

She doubted, however, that she'd ever be able to clear her head of the time spent in his room last night. Had he been playing along with her affection in order to distract her from his underhanded financial activities? If so, he'd done a skillful job of it.

Vivian was taking the Johnsons' coats to hang them on the hall rack. Aunt Shirley urged them to leave their snowy boots on a mat by the door and then rushed away to get some slippers for their guests.

Ruth wondered if the rest of the family knew there was a shyster in their midst. As they all headed into the parlor, she attempted to study their faces. Vivian and Aunt Shirley obviously had knowledge of Tucker's secretive goings-on. Aunt Ada and Uncle Oren were busy asking the couple about their drive back from Kentucky. Boris contemplated aloud the potential causes of their mechanical problems. Eldon and Rosemary busied themselves with arranging pillows on the sofa for their travel-weary guests. Brooke was babbling something about having once written a school report on Kentucky. And Dewey had plastered on a dry smile that camouflaged whatever emotions he might be experiencing at the moment. All were pointedly avoiding her gaze as they focused their attention elsewhere.

Tucker was the only one who wasn't wearing a guilty face. Perhaps he'd had so much practice bilking his victims that his conscience no longer bothered him.

They all knew. Everyone but her. Ruth sighed, wondering why her family had been so determined to ignore her warnings about the stranger in their midst.

Why had they been so willing to turn a blind eye while he swept in and took advantage of Aunt Shirley's trusting nature?

"Charles and I want to thank you for letting the kids stay with you over the holidays," Natalie Johnson said. "This has certainly been a hectic few days for all of us."

There would be no answers to Ruth's questions until she was able to pin Tucker down. Right now she needed to say her farewells to Nicky and Angie.

"It was truly our pleasure." Ruth scooped Angie onto her lap and pulled Nicky to her in a one-armed hug. To the children, she added, "Please come and see us again. Anytime."

If there was a house for them to come back to.

"Yes, indeed," piped in Aunt Shirley. "You're like members of our family now."

Ruth wondered if Aunt Shirley knew just how close she'd come to the truth with her innocent statement. The children had certainly come to seem like family to her. In fact, Ruth had secretly fantasized that the pair were her own children, and she had reveled in playing the role of surrogate mom to them. And even though Tucker was obviously not to be trusted in matters of business, he had been an outstanding paternal figure for the children. Having watched his playfulness and caring ways with Nicky and Angie, she found it ironic that a man who was so adamantly opposed to commitment should possess the very qualities that would make him a wonderful father.

"Can we bring Tucky, too?" Angie asked.

Ruth gave both her and the dog a hug. "Of course. He's a member of the family, too." If there was room for a con man in their family, then certainly they could include a beagle, as well.

The children giggled at that, but their parents' expressions went suddenly solemn. Charles Johnson leaned forward and rested his elbows on his knees. "Then I guess that makes what I have to say both good news and bad news."

Ruth felt her stomach constrict. She doubted she could handle any more bad news today. But Charles was already breaking it to them.

"Natalie and I *both* got jobs at the factory where I was interviewed. We'll be moving right away and starting work next week."

His wife beamed her pleasure. "I found us a house close to the plant and a nice school, and we'll have a fenced-in yard for Tucky!"

Angie bounced off Ruth's lap and danced in the middle of the floor while Nicky thrust his fist into the air and declared, "Yesss!" And the dog, charged up by the outpouring of excitement, bent himself nearly in half with full-body tail wags.

Tucker, along with her aunts, uncles, cousins and sister, applauded the news and high-fived the children.

Ruth seemed to be the only one who wasn't delighted about this new turn in their lives. She was happy for their good fortune, no doubt about that, but the prospect of possibly never seeing the children again left a vast, empty hole in her heart.

She had planned for this to be the most perfect Christmas ever. And now it was looking perfectly dreadful. Unwilling to put a damper on their happiness, Ruth tried to put on a brave face for the ecstatic family. Reminding herself the Johnsons' financial situation would be better in their new hometown, which would possibly enable her bright former student to attend college someday, she sought to think only of the benefits associated with their moving away. Moisture formed in the corner of her eye, and she tried to dab it away without calling attention to her action.

Tucker noticed. Wordlessly, he moved away from the rejoicing crowd and stood beside her, his arm draped around her shoulder.

First she'd lost the house, and now Nicky and Angie. She hoped with all her heart that bad news did not, as the superstition claimed, come in threes.

Despite the fact that Tucker was the cause of one of her losses today—namely, the house—she found his presence comforting. He seemed to understand why she'd grown suddenly quiet, and she was grateful that he didn't try to dismiss her pain as sentimental or selfish.

"Hang in there," he said in a low voice that only she could hear. "Your turn will come."

Yes, her turn would come. But had he read her mind about wanting children of her own? Or was he referring to the fact that she, too, would soon be leaving Willow Glen Plantation forever?

After the children had left with their parents, most of the Babcock clan escaped to parts unknown. Apparently, they didn't want to stick around for the showdown. Tucker and the two main culprits, Aunt Shirley and Vivian, remained. And Brooke, who was pretending to be engrossed in a teen fashion magazine in hopes of seeing some fireworks.

Ruth didn't really want an audience, especially not

one that was supportive of the man who'd caused so many problems in the short time he'd been here. A sense of fairness reminded her that he'd also been plenty helpful as well...to her entire family, to Nicky and Angie and to Ruth. But that wasn't what they were here to discuss right now.

Tucker was seated on the loveseat in the parlor. Since the others had dispersed to the other sofa and a wing-back chair, that left the spot beside him open. Rather than sink onto the comfortable cushion where he would naturally tower over her, she perched on the arm of the furniture. Anything to give her a little more leverage and a little more distance when dealing with this impossible man.

"At this point, I'm thinking I should follow what was my first impulse and ask you to go back where you came from," she told him. If she had been wise enough to follow those protective instincts, she would never have fallen in love with a man who would not be there for her. A man who would take what he could and then leave. Well, he'd already taken everything he could get—Aunt Shirley's house and Ruth's heart— and now it was time for him to go before he hurt them any further.

Tucker sprawled back against the loveseat as if to show that he wasn't thinking of going anywhere anytime soon. He twisted his mouth to one side as he took in what she said. "You can't ask me to leave," he said with finality. "This is my house."

His tone was not braggy...just matter-of-fact. She had to give him credit for not crowing about the heist he'd manipulated.

Clutching the official-looking document she'd

picked up earlier, she decided it didn't have to remain so. She could have a say in this matter, after all. "I have the paperwork," she said, holding it up for him to see. "If I tear up the deed, then you don't have diddly."

He exhaled a patient sigh. "Your aunt and I already filed it at the courthouse. It's a simple matter to get another copy." Leaning forward, he braced a hand on the empty cushion beside him. "Ruth, this is not what you think. If you'd give me a moment to explain—"

"No." Ruth propelled herself off the loveseat arm, refusing to hear the pretty words that had already seduced her family. Pacing the floor and slapping the deed against her thigh, she turned to her aunt. "How could you have done such a thing? How could you let a stranger come into your house and just take it away from you?"

Brooke noisily flipped a page in her magazine.

Ruth directed her next question to Vivian. "And how could you have let her? Encouraged her, even?"

"Aunt Shirley has a mind of her own," her sister said. "Besides, it was for a good reason."

Annoyed, Ruth spun away. There was just no getting through to them. Charmed by Tucker's good looks and sweet manner—and who knew what else, as far as Vivian was concerned—they had apparently taken whatever he said as gospel truth.

Aunt Shirley straightened a crocheted doily on the arm of the chair in which she sat. "I'll tell you how I could do such a thing. When I announced that this would be our last family reunion in this house, you refused to hear what I was saying." Now she smoothed a fold in her floral skirt. "It wasn't because

I was tired of the reunions or that they were too much work.''

"It wasn't?" Ruth stopped her pacing and knelt beside her aunt's chair. She touched the gnarled fingers of the woman who had braided her hair, demonstrated cooking techniques and admonished her over the years.

"No, it wasn't because of the work or energy involved." Shirley gave her hand a gentle squeeze. "I've been feeling restless lately. I'm getting older, Ruth, and there's a lot I want to see and do before I croak.''

Vivian sat up straight. "Aunt Shirley!"

"But what does that have to do with our reunions? And the house?" Ruth asked, ignoring her sister's outburst.

"I want to see the world beyond Willow Glen. When I hurt my hip and had difficulty climbing the stairs, it made me realize how quickly time is passing. I've been giving a lot of thought to buying a big, fancy motor home and taking off with Boris on a cross-country trip." She sat up straighter and smiled. "One of the first things we're going to do is see Wayne Newton perform in Las Vegas. That man is such a hunk...but don't you dare tell Boris I said so.''

Ruth balanced on the balls of her feet, taking all this in.

"I know you love this old house," Shirley continued, "but I can't afford to keep it up and travel, too. And you can't afford to buy it on a teacher's salary. So I did the next best thing and sold it to Cousin Tucker for a fair price." She flashed a benevolent smile across the room at him. "Besides, he has some very interesting plans for it."

By now, Brooke had dropped the magazine and all pretense of being interested in its articles.

"Really?" Ruth rose to her feet and crossed the room. Seating herself beside Tucker, she leaned one arm against the back of the loveseat. Now they were finally getting down to the nitty-gritty. "What exactly *are* your plans?"

He squirmed, confirming her suspicions. "Actually," he said, running a nervous hand across his temple, "I bought it for you."

Ruth felt her mouth gape. Aware that everyone in the room had turned to her, watching for her reaction, she clamped her lips together. It was clear they were all thinking the same thing—that Tucker's plans for the house included Ruth...and marriage.

At first she was skeptical. But Aunt Shirley was nodding and smiling, with Vivian mimicking her actions.

"Why else did you think Cousin Tucker and I were having all those secret conversations?" Vivian asked. "It was all we could do to keep you from finding out what was going on."

"But why didn't you just tell me?"

Vivian snorted in a most unVivian-like fashion. "Yeah, right. Like you'd have gone along with it!"

"You didn't exactly take kindly to me at first," Tucker clarified.

They were right. She hadn't been open-minded about his presence in the house. In fact, she'd believed he was up to no good, right from the start. If they'd come to her with such a plan, she would have vetoed the sale immediately.

As if it had turned to liquid, Ruth felt her heart soften. Her hopes rose even further when she realized Tucker's interest in her sister had been business related.

Ruth had fallen for their unexpected guest immediately—and resisted the attraction. Perhaps he, too, had automatically been resisting an involvement with her. Perhaps that was why he had claimed last night that he wasn't ready to offer her a commitment. Things had, after all, developed very quickly. Perhaps, like herself, he had been sorting through his jumbled emotions.

Brooke got up from where she'd been sitting, and her magazine fell to the floor. "This is so romantic!" she cried, clapping her hands to her cheeks. "Before long, you two will fill this whole house with babies."

Turning to look at the man who was making her dreams come true, Ruth was surprised to see that he'd gone a chalky gray. Considering the weak twist of his mouth and the way he clutched his side, she wondered if he might be getting sick to his stomach.

He met her gaze, and his complexion turned clammier still.

She reached out toward him, concerned that he may have picked up a virus or eaten something that disagreed with him. "Tucker, are you all right?"

"No," he said, "I'm not." And without further explanation, he rushed from the room.

Chapter Ten

Tucker didn't stop until he was out on the front porch where the winter air slapped him in the face. His sinuses stung as he gulped the bitter air. Bracing himself against the porch rail, he considered the implications of what had just taken place. Of what had been taking place since he'd first returned to Willow Glen Plantation.

Attachments had formed in the short time he'd been here. Not only for the family as a whole, but for Ruth in particular. His heartstrings had woven themselves around her and were tying a knot that threatened to strangle him. He'd been in this position before—caring about someone special—and he'd seen how much it could hurt. He couldn't allow himself to risk another loss.

But Ruth had misread his intentions. It was clear, especially after their time together in his room last night, that she wanted there to be something more between them. And today she'd totally misunderstood what he'd meant to do about the house.

He ran a hand along the back of his neck. The kids probably had something to do with that. He could tell she'd started to consider them her own family, and she'd begun looking at him as if he were the paternal one of the group. She'd been devastated when she learned the kids were moving to Kentucky. And he suspected she was now latching on to him as a means of helping her replace the brood she'd lost.

He hated to crush her ambitions, but he hated even more for her to be carrying false hopes. Hopes that included him. He was going to have to tell her the truth.

The front door opened, and he knew without looking who it must be.

"Tucker?"

His back still turned to her, he cleared his throat as he considered how he would break the news. And her heart.

"Are you all right?" Her voice was soft and calm, the same kind of voice she would use if one of the children were sick or injured.

Turning around, he leaned against the post. The carved wood dug into his back, but he didn't care. He considered it punishment for the pain he was about to inflict on Ruth.

"Yeah, I just needed some fresh air." He studied her, watching the play of emotions across her face. She'd make a terrible poker player. "I also need to clear up what the deal is about the house."

She stepped closer, her face relaxing into a soft smile. Tucker stopped her with an outstretched palm.

"That night your aunt bruised her hip, she told me about her plans to go traveling with Boris. She also told me that you would be devastated if you no longer had a place to hold the family reunion."

She gave a small nod, encouraging him to continue.

"And since I have such a sentimental attachment to this place, I couldn't stand the thought of it being sold to strangers again."

He moved to one side, making room for her to join him by the porch rail. And he tried not to notice the shiver that shook her narrow shoulders. Unfortunately, concern won out over common sense, and he put an arm around her to warm her. He only hoped she wouldn't misread this gesture, as well. When she snuggled comfortably against him, he knew that once again he'd made the wrong move.

"So we agreed—the family and I—that I would buy the house and allow you to continue living in it."

Her countenance lifted, and she smiled up at him as she anticipated what he was about to say next. He'd have to hurry and spit out the truth before she decided on bridesmaid dresses and china patterns.

"I'll be happy to set up some affordable rent payments."

Confusion flickered across her face. Tucker turned away and stared at the brass spittoon that served as an ashtray beside the front door. He needed to do this quickly…like ripping a bandage off. It would hurt like hell at first, but the pain wouldn't last as long as if he did it slowly.

"And if you should marry—say, a fellow school-teacher or the principal or some other nice guy—and you and your husband want to buy the house, you can have it for the same price I paid.''

She moved away from him, and her shivering increased. ''My husband and I?''

He nodded. ''I like you a lot, Ruth.'' *Like* didn't even begin to describe how he felt about her.

''I sense a 'but' in there.'' Her voice was flat, as if it'd had to squeeze past a lump in her throat.

''But we have different goals. Different needs. I made a mistake when I came here, getting so involved with your family even when I knew I should be keeping my distance.'' He sighed. ''I can't straddle the fence anymore. I can't keep trying to blend two worlds that weren't meant to be together.''

''I'm scared, too. I've never fallen so hard or so fast before.'' She paced the porch, avoiding the spot where partially melted snow was now starting to freeze. Then she stopped and faced him directly. ''I understand your reluctance to commit yourself to a new relationship. But life has to go on, Tucker. You have to take a chance sometimes. Or else you'll end up a bitter, lonely old man.''

Tucker bit down on the inside of his lip. He couldn't argue with what she said. But he couldn't bring himself to agree with her, either. ''This isn't a good time for either of us to be discussing this. You're missing the children, and that's affecting how you feel. Whatever affections you have for me may be simply a misplaced wish for a family of your own.''

She ceased her pacing and squinted her eyes at him in silent refute. ''What would your friend Chris say if he could see you now? Would he approve of you throwing away something that's good in your life?

Something that makes you—makes both of us—happy?''

Jamming his hands in his pockets, he turned his shoulder to her. The only thing that had come of this discussion—of the entire time he'd spent here at Willow Glen Plantation—was more hurt feelings.

''Chris isn't here now.''

''And that's the root of the problem, isn't it?'' she asked softly. ''You've lost someone you loved, and now you're afraid to love again. I never figured you for a coward, Tucker Maddock.''

''We both should have listened to our first instincts,'' he told her. ''It would have spared us both a lot of pain.''

''Pain comes with growth. And with living a full, complete life.''

Not true. In this case, pain was a warning. Just as the heat of a flame cautioned them to keep a safe distance. Having already been singed by the fire, it was a little late to be heeding the alarm. But it was far better to escape with some blackened edges than to stay and suffer the full consequences.

''I'm sorry,'' he said. Sorry he couldn't give her the promise of commitment she needed. Sorry they'd ever met and tasted the sweetness of the life they could never have. ''I think it would be best if I go now.''

He stepped past her and entered the house for the final time. Her stricken expression followed him as he took the stairs two at a time, and it stayed with him while he haphazardly threw his belongings into his battered duffel bag.

Unable to humiliate herself any further by begging him to stay, Ruth watched from the kitchen window as Tucker's small black car pulled out of the driveway. The rest of the family had rallied around, giving him a hero's send-off and urging him to come back for a visit anytime he wished.

They were still gathered in the foyer, waving their good-byes while the open door sent a draft through the entire house and into Ruth's soul. She rubbed her arms and blinked back a tear that had formed.

Vivian came up from behind and watched over her shoulder as Tucker's hand emerged from his car window and waved them all farewell. She could tell it was Vivian just by the tiny whiff of perfume that drifted toward her. *Come Hither.*

Ruth pinched herself in penance for the unkind thought. Her sister's involvement with Tucker had only been for Ruth's benefit. And she appreciated what she'd tried to do. But she still couldn't bring herself to turn away from the window, even after Tucker's car had gone out of sight down the street.

"So, you're throwing this one away, too?" Vivian asked.

Ruth moved her hands to her hips and spun around in response to the confrontational tone in her sister's voice. "What are you talking about?"

"You're too picky. You date a guy awhile, and then after you decide he isn't perfect enough, you dump him on me." She flipped a blond tendril behind her shoulder. "This time, though, you seem to have broken the pattern."

"I've never dumped anyone on you!" First there'd been Tucker's crazy logic about why he couldn't stay, and now this. She had no idea why her sister was bringing up her past boyfriends, but since she had, Ruth intended to set the record straight. "You were always on the sidelines, waiting to move in for the kill."

Vivian laughed, the sound decidedly unhumorous. "Yeah, right. Like I'd be interested in those guys. I hate to tell you, sis, but until Tucker, your taste in men really stunk."

The day was taking a toll on her. Ruth moved to the table and slid into one of the chairs. "Then why did you go out with them?"

Vivian shrugged and joined her at the table, resting one elbow on the tatted cloth and her chin on her hand. "You seemed so distressed, like you didn't know how to get rid of them. So I just tried to do you a favor. What else could I do?" she said with a shrug. "You practically pushed them into my arms."

It was a good thing Ruth was already sitting. Otherwise the spinning room would have sent her reeling. Vivian actually thought she had passed those boyfriends off to her? Because she wanted to get rid of them?

She slumped in the chair. If Aunt Shirley were in here, she'd be scolding her to sit up straight. But right now, Ruth doubted she had the strength to pull herself upright. She'd had so much to deal with already today, and now Vivian was throwing another bomb at her.

When she considered what the other woman had said, though, she had to admit that she hadn't really cared much for any of those former dates. If those boys—and later men—had their heads turned by the curvy blonde, it may have been because Ruth had already made it clear through her actions that she wasn't interested in developing the relationship any further.

Vivian heaved a wistful sigh. "Now, Tucker's one man I wouldn't mind taking off your hands. Too bad he's head-over-heels crazy for you."

Ruth felt her eyes mist up again. "If that's true, then why did he just leave?"

"He's an idiot. All men are idiots." Straightening in her chair, Vivian leaned forward and touched Ruth's arm. "And they're even worse when they're in love."

He was doing what was best for both of them. That was what Tucker kept telling himself with each tenth-mile turn of the odometer. The problem was that the memory of the pained lines of Ruth's beautiful face tormented him as he drove toward the edge of town.

Blinking away the image, he focused his attention on maneuvering through the slush. The afternoon sun had softened the snow, but now the temperatures were dipping, and patches of newly forming ice slowed his getaway.

He wanted to go back. It was craziness to think such a thing. Such a move would be wrong for both of them. They'd only known each other a short time. And, as he'd told her earlier, they each had different needs. Right now, his need was to retreat to the safety of his empty apartment where no one awaited his return and there were no emotional ties that put his heart at risk.

As he turned right onto Pendleton Avenue, the duffel bag on the passenger seat overturned, spilling some of its contents. In his haste to flee Willow Glen Plantation, he hadn't bothered to close the zipper. And now his Christmas gifts graced the leather upholstery.

Grabbing a couple, he pushed them back into the bag. But when his fingers touched the smooth silk one, he thought how it reminded him of the giver. The shimmery charcoal-gray background brought to mind the soft gray sweater she'd been wearing last night when she came to his room. And the varying shades of gold and yellow in the center made him think of how she had brightened his mood whenever she'd walked into the room.

The light ahead turned yellow, and Tucker came to a careful stop. Driving conditions were becoming treacherous, and the small car didn't have much weight to give it traction.

Pushing Ruth's tie aside, but still leaving it out where he could look at it occasionally during the ride home, he gathered up some of the others and pushed them back into the bag.

In all the years he'd worked in an office, Tucker had considered this part of business attire as little more than a decorative noose. He'd always hated the way they pinched his neck, but Ruth's sister had shown him how to wrap the knot so that it wouldn't bind. A grin pulled up at the corners of his mouth as he recalled Ruth's reaction when Vivian had reached around him and guided his fingers in demonstration.

These weren't just neckties, he realized. The light turned green, and he eased away from the intersection. They represented family ties. The very ties that he was trying to run away from. Like the strips of cloth that would remind him, whenever he wore them, of the special people who had briefly entered his life, he was taking back a piece of each of them. The neckties would eventually fray and be discarded after a time, but the family ties would stay with him long afterward, no matter how hard he tried to purge them from his memory.

They would stay with him forever. And perhaps even longer.

The stocking Aunt Ada had made for him was still hanging from the mantel…left behind like his rebellious heart. Like it or not, he was a member of their family. And they were his family.

Like a necktie that was knotted improperly, those family ties tugged at him…pulling his heart and pinching his conscience until he couldn't stand it any longer. Briefly, he considered tossing his brightly colored gifts out the window to rid himself of the unwanted feelings that nagged at his long-held beliefs, undermining his willpower. But discarding the material ties would not sever the emotional bonds that he'd formed over the past week and a half.

He wanted to go back. No, strike that. His heart wanted to go back. Tucker's common sense urged him to keep driving.

He switched on the radio. Maybe a rousing country tune would distract him from his traitorous feelings.

Why did you leave me high and dry? a woman's voice beseeched. *I feel lower than a snake's belly and I'm drenched with all my tears.*

Tucker ground his teeth and turned the radio knob until it clicked off. He'd made Ruth feel bad, he acknowledged. It wasn't her fault she'd fallen for such a jerk as himself. And it wasn't his fault that he wanted to be with the tiny woman who had so quickly melted the ice around his heart and warmed it with her love.

A cloud shifted, and a ray of sunlight streaked downward through the sky, lighting up the patches of crusty snow that remained. The illumination spread to Tucker's heart as he realized what a fool he'd been.

All this time he'd been seeking to avoid the inevitable pain of losing someone he loved. And now, driving away from Willow Glen Plantation, he himself was causing the loss this time.

There were no guarantees in life. The Johnsons, for instance, could get laid off from their new jobs. But that possibility wasn't keeping them from enjoying the anticipation of their newfound prosperity. Or from doing what they could to make their children's lives better in the meantime.

For the first time, Tucker realized that he had allowed himself to die with the Newlands. He had been going through his daily routines like a zombie, his heart as cold as if he were in the grave with them.

But Ruth had changed that. Because of her, he couldn't go back to his life as it had been before. Now that she had touched his life, he couldn't imagine going a day—much less forever—without seeing her radiant smile, hearing her spontaneous laughter or tasting her warm, honey-sweet lips. His misery came not from another lousy Christmas; rather, he'd made his own fears come true. He couldn't allow himself to lose another loved one.

Old habits were taking him home…to a city and lifestyle he hated and away from the only woman he'd ever loved. It was about time he started forming some new habits.

Tucker let up on the gas. The interstate on-ramp was about a mile ahead. But up on the left, just beyond the crossroad, beckoned a gas station where he could turn around.

And go home. To his family.

He slowed the car just as he crossed Harmony Hill Road. But a silver foreign car coming down the incline to his left skidded on a patch of ice, careering sideways past the stop sign. When it plowed into the intersection, Tucker instinctively turned his body and flung up an arm as he braced for the impact.

Tucker leaned back against the paper-covered pillow on the examining table and waited for the nurse to return with the release papers for him to sign.

There was a cast on his foot, and bandages covered his arm. It could have been worse, he supposed, and was instantly grateful it hadn't been. It already annoyed him beyond words that this side trip to the emergency room had slowed his return to Ruth. The broken bone in his foot and the numerous glass cuts on his elbow and forearm hurt far less than having to wait even another few minutes to see the woman he loved. The woman he wanted to share a thousand Christmases with.

The stout young nurse returned with a clipboard and pen and laid them on his lap. "Who's coming to pick you up?"

"Uh, I don't..." His hand shook, and he put down the pen. "No one knows I'm here."

"Would you like me to call someone for you?" Previously her attitude had been brisk. But now the woman seemed to soften as she waited for his reply.

What a difference a few days made. If this accident had happened two weeks ago—before he met Ruth—he would have had to call on his secretary or a co-worker to give him a ride home. But now... Now he wanted to see Ruth even more than he wanted to take his next breath.

"Ruth Marsh," he said with a nod of his head, and gave the woman her phone number.

And then he waited, wondering if she could ever forgive him for his stupidity. Since he had refused to stay at Willow Glen Plantation with her, would she now refuse to come to him? He wouldn't blame her if she turned her back on him, just as he had done to her.

In just a matter of minutes, the examining room overflowed with Babcock family members. Taking care not to jostle his leg, Ruth perched on the gurney beside him and held his uninjured hand. Was it his imagination, or had she been crying?

"It's a wonder we made it here alive," Uncle Oren announced from behind her. "Our little Ruth drove like a maniac to get here."

"Nonsense! She drove very carefully," Aunt Shirley said in her defense. "She just didn't take any longer than was absolutely necessary."

If Ruth was embarrassed at having been exposed, she didn't show it. All of her attention was focused on him. "Is there anyone back home you need to call?" she asked. "Do you have any family?"

Not unless they counted the apartment superintendent who had agreed to keep an eye on his place while he was gone. Tucker slowly shook his head.

She seemed so sad for him. A sea of faces milled

around him, each gazing at him with concern and love. The positive feelings that they surrounded him with were multiplied in his heart, which seemed to be overflowing at the moment. And he reconsidered his answer to her question.

"Yes, I do have family. You." He slipped his arm around her waist and nodded toward the people who had accepted him so unconditionally. "All of you."

To his immense relief, she smiled her acknowledgment and leaned forward to kiss him. When her soft skin met his, Tucker forgot about everything but the whirling emotions she stirred in his soul. Tightening his arm around her, he wanted to hold her like this always. When he kissed her in return, he claimed her love with every fiber of his being. All the fears he'd harbored no longer seemed important. The only thing that mattered was holding on to her and savoring every minute with her…for the rest of his life.

"Let's make our family ties official," he said. "Marry me, Ruth. And make me the happiest man on earth."

When Ruth said yes, the entire family cheered.

Epilogue

The chapel in Willow Glen was filled to the rafters with family, friends and well-wishers. Tiny white Christmas lights graced the exit at the front of the church where Ruth and Tucker would soon walk out arm in arm, and the candle stands sported running cedar with miniature red silk balls. Attached to the chandelier above them, a sprig of mistletoe—or was it holly?—awaited the completion of their vows.

The past year had been a flurry of activity as Tucker wrapped up his obligations in Alexandria and started his own consulting firm in neighboring Portsmouth. Boris and Aunt Shirley had driven their new motor home to Las Vegas where they tied the knot. And Ruth had dealt with the thousands of details involved in planning a big wedding. Ultimately, she and Tucker had decided that a holiday wedding would set the tone for future happy Christmases together.

Behind Tucker and Ruth, the pews on both sides

were tightly packed despite the fact that today was Christmas. The groom's side consisted of some of his friends and co-workers, and the rest of the seats were filled with Ruth's family.

Little Angie fidgeted beside Brooke, bouncing the empty rose-petal basket against her lifted knee. Her brother, outfitted in an usher's tux and standing to the right of Tucker, whispered an admonition to his sister to settle down.

Tucker merely laughed at the sibling squabble. Ruth had never seen him look more dashing. Or happier.

Gazing up at the man who stood beside her at the altar, she gave thanks for the Christmas miracle that had brought him into her life one short year ago. His handsome face curved into a smile.

"You grow more beautiful every day," he told her. Seeing herself reflected in his eyes, she no longer felt plain or ordinary...not even standing beside her eye-dazzling sister who served as the maid of honor.

The minister cleared his throat and began the ceremony. Ruth had memorized the vows she'd written, but she touched the small "cheat sheet" tucked in the bouquet for reassurance. Tucker reached over and squeezed her hand.

After some of the solemnities were out of the way, the preacher stepped back and addressed the audience. "Who gives this woman?"

Ruth cringed. She had never particularly liked that part of the service and had intended to take it out during the planning of the wedding. Unfortunately, it had slipped her mind during the confusion of having the house filled with out-of-town relatives.

A commotion sounded behind her as shoes scuffed

and stiff new dresses crinkled with a mass movement. Curious, she looked behind her to see that every one of her family members had risen from their seats. Her sister, aunts, uncles, cousins and great-relatives responded in well-rehearsed unison, "We all do."

She lifted a hand to her face. When Tucker leaned close to see what was the matter, she whispered, "I'm so embarrassed."

"Don't be," he said with a loving squeeze of her shoulder. "I wouldn't have it any other way."

As for Ruth, she really wouldn't, either. Her Christmas wish had come true. Her family was finally complete.

And this was the most perfect Christmas ever.

* * * * *

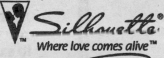

WITH HARLEQUIN AND SILHOUETTE

There's a romance to fit your every mood.

Passion

Harlequin Temptation

Harlequin Presents

Silhouette Desire

Pure Romance

Harlequin Romance

Silhouette Romance

Home & Family

Harlequin
American Romance

Silhouette
Special Edition

A Longer Story With More

Harlequin
Superromance

Suspense & Adventure

Harlequin Intrigue

Silhouette Intimate Moments

Humor

Harlequin Duets

Historical

Harlequin Historicals

Special Releases

Other great
romances
to explore

THE F⬡RTUNES OF TEXAS

invite you to a memorable Christmas celebration in

Gifts of F⬡RTUNE

Patriarch Ryan Fortune has met death head-on and now he has a special gift for each of the four honorable individuals who stood by him in his hour of need. This holiday collection contains stories by three of your most beloved authors.

THE HOLIDAY HEIR
by Barbara Boswell

THE CHRISTMAS HOUSE
by Jennifer Greene

MAGGIE'S MIRACLE
by Jackie Merritt

And be sure to watch for **Did You Say Twins?!** by Maureen Child, the exciting conclusion to the *Fortunes of Texas: The Lost Heirs* miniseries, coming only to Silhouette Desire in December 2001.

Don't miss these unforgettable romances... available at your favorite retail outlet.

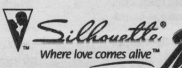

Silhouette®
Where love comes alive™

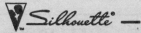